Brief II
Candle

Kate Pennington

*Hodder
Children's
Books*

A division of Hodder Headline Limited

A Catalogue record for this book is available from the British Library

ISBN 0 340 87370 1

Typeset in Garamond by Avon DataSet Ltd,
Bidford-on-Avon, Warwickshire

Printed and bound in Great Britain by
Clays Ltd, St Ives PLC, Bungay, Suffolk

The paper and board used in this paperback by Hodder Children's Books
are natural recyclable products made from wood grown in sustainable forests.
The manufacturing processes conform to the environmental
regulations of the country of origin.

Hodder Children's Books
a division of Hodder Headline Limited
338 Euston Road
London NW1 3BH

For my mother and father,
who gave me a wonderful Yorkshire childhood.

Tabitha Ackroyd's account, summer, 1854

I came to the parsonage in the summer of 1825, and have remained here these thirty years, so it has not proved a bad life, though many times my heart has ached.

I recall the four children were always under my feet. I could not bake bread nor cook their dinner without them tumbling into the kitchen, playing their games.

Such games as you never beheld – of Islanders, six miles high, and of entire new worlds conjured up from a box of toy soldiers. They played so hard that oftentimes I supposed them out of their wits. Why, in the winters I would keep candles from them so that they must go to bed and leave off their foolishness.

They had no mother, poor lambs, and so they huddled together for warmth. They clung tight while their aunt, Miss Branwell, kept to her room and their father, my employer, went about his parish.

Charlotte was the eldest, only seven years of age in my first summer here, and I found her a sickly, near-sighted girl when she and Emily returned from the school that had killed their two older sisters – Maria and Elizabeth. They died of the consumption at Cowan Bridge.

Branwell came next in line. Little Bany with his shock of red hair. Charlotte took great care of him, she was his little mother.

Then Emily.

And then Anne with her stammer, trying to keep pace with her elders.

You ask me about Emily.

She spoke with an Irish brogue, which she had from her father. She would help me turn and hem garments. She made her own bed and swept the carpets. Is that what you wish to hear?

She never laid fires or polished the grate, which was my task, the three girls being brought up as young ladies on the insistence of their aunt. I had help from the village one day a week in the wash-house, and that was all.

Emily, you say again? She would walk on the moor with her dogs. She would make her little books with Anne.

The stories? I have little recollection – only that the world they invented was called Gondal and there were thrones of gold with diamond canopies, towns of glass, and suchlike nonsense.

But I would tell her, and she would listen, of the days in these hollows before the mills came with their high chimneys. I would tell her of the packhorses carrying wool and stone into Lancashire. There were fairies by the becks then, and when the morning mist cleared you could see their rings.

Why, my own mother, when I was a child, came running in at the edge of dark, flayed out of her wits, saying that she had seen a fairy, and that was the last one ever seen in this country – in a lonely spot thick with oak and nut trees.

Emily loved to hear such tales, as children do.

What else, besides the learning of her lessons in geography and history?

Only that she never spoke willingly to strangers.

When forced to leave her home, she fell ill and almost died.

She is gone now, however, and I pray that she is with God, and that her slumbers are peaceful under this quiet earth.

Report on Emily Bronte, on her admittance to Cowan Bridge School, aged six, November 1825

Reads very prettily.

From Charlotte Bronte's preface to *Wuthering Heights*, 1851

My sister, Emily, loved the moors ... They were far more to her than mere spectacle; they were what she lived in and by ... She found in the bleak solitude many and dear delights; and not the least and best loved was – liberty.

One

'Am I free to go now?' Emily demanded.

Tabby looked up from the steaming copper where she and Sally Mosley stirred the weekly wash. 'Have you peeled the potatoes?' she asked.

'Done!' Emily cried.

'Have you tidied the parlour?'

'No, but Anne is to take a broom to the carpet, and Charlotte has cleared away her paints.' Emily shifted restlessly from one foot to the other. 'Tabby, please say I may go out with Captain!'

The parsonage servant heaved at the laundry with a long pole. 'Go then!'

So Emily retreated from the wash-house with rising spirits. 'No more drudgery!' she told her beloved dog, taking a stout leather leash from the hook on the kitchen door. 'Aunt is reading upstairs and will not mind if I leave off my sewing until after dinner.'

The dog bounded out into the yard and up onto the field behind the house. A pair of plovers started out of the long grass and flew up into the cloudy sky. Soon

Emily followed, running after Captain until they reached the stone stile at the top of the field. There, a slight, red-headed figure appeared from behind the wall, leaping into view with a stout stick held aloft. 'Hold!' it cried.

Emily sighed and stood back. 'Branwell, you startled us.'

'You must give way to Alexander Soult, son of Marshal Soult, friend to the great Emperor Napoleon!'

'Come down then,' Emily conceded, watching her brother jump to the ground. 'Run to Charlotte and tell her I am gone with Captain up to the waterfalls, where she may find me once she has finished with her drawing.'

Branwell gave a doubtful glance at the grey skies. 'It will rain,' he predicted.

'Let it.'

'Your shoes will be wet. Aunt will scold.'

'Let her.' Squeezing past her killjoy brother and eager to stride out into the hills, Emily heaved Captain into her arms and climbed the stile. She set him down in the rough heather on the far side. 'Today is my birthday. Aunt will not scold too hard nor too long.'

'Yes, today is your fourteenth birthday and you must play the young lady, not run roaming onto the moors like a gypsy!' Branwell countered, with a thrust of his sword. 'This evening, you are to accompany me, Young

Soult, to meet Young Murat and Young Ney at the palace of my friend, Young Lucien Bonaparte!'

'And I will!' Emily promised, her voice lost in the wind as she raced off.

Ahead of her, Captain raised more birds – pheasants this time – throwing back his head and barking wildly. The pheasants clattered skyward, trailing their long tails in the grass and beating their heavy wings.

Today is my birthday! Emily repeated to herself. I have life and liberty, and no man may bind me!

Emily Jane Brontë's Diary Paper, July 1832

I fed Captain, Emerald and Snowflake.

This afternoon Captain and I went up to the waterfall and waited for Charlotte, who did not come.

Anne and I made apple pudding with Tabby. I peeled the apples. Aunt came into the kitchen just now and said I peeled apples poorly and that I should never make a pudding like Tabby did.

Papa received a letter from Mr W of Halifax who will teach Branwell to paint in oils. He said, 'Here, Branwell, now you see I am prepared to turn you into a fine artist with the help of Mr W.'

Anne and I have not done our lessons, being much taken up with the Gondalians' exploration of Gaaldine. The natives of that place are offering resistance, but as yet there is no threat to the Emperor nor to the Empress herself.

Charlotte looks in a mirror and complains of her lack of stature. 'I am as short and dumpy as ever,' she says. On Tuesday next we shall have all the female teachers of the Sunday school to tea. I shall escape to Top Withens.

This is my birthday. Anne and I wonder what we shall be like and where we shall be this day four years hence. Anne says in this drawing room, comfortable, and I hope it shall be so. Hoping we shall all be well at that time, I close this paper.

Two

Charlotte laboured over her painting while Emily wrote her diary.

July had ended, and with August came the purple bloom of heather on the moor behind the parsonage.

'I am afraid that Branwell does not pay enough attention to Mr Whitehouse's advice over applying the paint to a prepared canvas,' Charlotte said quietly. Her brushstrokes were fine and delicate as she completed the watercolour portrait of the Empress Zenobia. She concentrated on the large, clear eyes, then touched up the curls that clustered around her heroine's graceful neck.

'Branwell takes no one's advice,' Emily replied. She looked up impatiently at the rain-spattered window pane. At her feet Captain twitched in his sleep.

'I long to be a painter, and to be given the chance to go to London.' Sighing, Charlotte put down her brushes and contemplated the small, finished portrait.

'And leave home?' Emily asked with a shake of her head. 'London is full of strangers, and noise and dark

streets like warrens running here and there. I should not like it.'

'Emily, have you no wish to break out from this quiet life, not even in your most secret heart?' Charlotte persisted.

'Not I.'

Another sigh from Charlotte brought Anne into the cramped bedroom at the head of the stairs where the two girls worked and talked. 'What is the matter, Charlotte?' the youngest sister asked.

'Nothing, Anne. Nothing that can be remedied at any rate. Unless you can transform me into a man and make for me a man's way in the world!'

'Charlotte wishes to flee the nest,' Emily said, matter of fact. 'She wishes for Branwell's opportunities, to see London and the great galleries. Did you know, Anne, that our sister would be a famous painter and have her pictures hung in the homes of the rich and powerful?'

'I did not say so,' Charlotte argued with a blush.

Anne's frown lifted. 'Then you will not leave us again?' She recalled Charlotte's departure for Mirfield in the covered cart some eighteen months previously. It had been a bitter January morning, scarcely light, and the frost had glittered on the cobbled surface of Haworth's steep hill. The house had seemed strange without her.

'Not unless you can work the magic I mentioned

before.' Quietly Charlotte rose to clear away her paints from the deep windowsill. 'No, I fear we sisters are condemned to remain here in this house, overlooking these gravestones, for the rest of our lives!'

Emily went to the window and gazed out. Rain had darkened the flat slabs of stone which covered the graves so that they seemed black. The arms of the tall crosses dripped soundlessly. Would there be a chance of taking a walk after supper, she wondered.

Anne took up Charlotte's painting. 'Zenobia is even more beautiful than you describe her. Emily, we must make a play where our heroine is as brilliant. Her eyes must sparkle like diamonds, her hair must be black as Whitby jet!'

'And our hero?' Emily asked, allowing Anne space at the window.

'Brave and strong,' Anne replied. 'An adventurer.'

'A man of passion?'

'A dark man disguised under a monk's hood, travelling among tall towers, between great pillars, under gloomy skies!' Anne sailed on the wings of fantasy, her pretty face alive with excitement.

'An exile?' Emily prompted.

Anne nodded. 'Cast out from his dear home, condemned to wander alone and unhappy, seeking to regain his birthright!'

Emily's gaze grew soft and she smiled. 'Perfect!'

From downstairs Tabby's loud voice broke the spell. 'Children!' she called. 'Master's home. I see him shaking off his coat in the church porch. Will you clear away your mess and come down!'

'We will, Tabby!' they promised.

Today was the day of the month when Papa returned from Keighley with the latest periodicals. There would be news from the wider world to be shared over a boiled beef supper, and an idea that might shape Charlotte's future if the seed were to take hold and germinate.

'You could be a teacher,' Mr Brontë suggested. 'You are a clever girl, and neat in your ways. You would be an asset in any school.'

Charlotte sat at the table grim-faced and pale.

Her father peered at her over his spectacles. Above his starched white cravat his expression was alert, his hooked nose giving him the aspect of one of Emily's tame hawks. 'Well, Charlotte?'

'I had not thought to teach.' She shivered at the thought. To stand before a group of girls and be studied – to have her every feature dissected and made the subject of jest. How small she is, and how stunted! Her eyes are those of a blind mole. See how she squints through her glasses!

Emily sat fearfully at Charlotte's side. Charlotte was to be a teacher. If Papa suggested it, then it was already decided. And if Charlotte must take the course of duty, going out into the world to make a living, then it must follow that in due course Emily herself must do the same.

'You had not thought to do it, but what say you now?' their father insisted.

'I am not yet seventeen, Papa.'

In Emily too the notion of becoming a teacher evoked dread of the most intense kind – to stand before strangers and be scorned! She longed to leave the room, to be spared the torture of imagining.

Mr Brontë lowered his head. 'True, there is no need to hasten the event,' he conceded. 'I would keep you with us yet a while, my dear.'

Charlotte's eyes glistened with tears of relief. 'First I must learn French and music,' she murmured. 'I am not prepared.'

Beside her Emily still held her breath. Charlotte was to be a teacher, and herself and Anne after her. The certainty took hold, cold as ice.

That night Emily turned the pages of *Blackwood's Magazine* and found the words dry as dust, the events described there only shadows.

I have passed my fourteenth birthday and not spent a single night from home these past eight years. Long may it remain thus, she thought.

'You are too passionate,' Charlotte told Emily.

They had walked together to the waterfall above the village, through thick purple heather, with Captain running ahead.

Now they sat on the flat stone slab that bridged the fast-running stream. Emily dangled her bare feet in the cold water, while Charlotte rested her back against Emily's shoulder and stretched her legs sideways along the bridge.

'Better to be passionate than dry and rational,' Emily argued. 'What is there in the end except the life of feeling and imagination?'

Feeling that soared like the birds overhead, imagination that lifted you above the harsh world.

'Duty,' Charlotte said dully. 'Besides passion there is duty – doing what we ought, fulfilling a task, working for others.'

Emily sat a while and let the water wash around her ankles. 'Ah!' she said quietly.

'Duty is what will drive me back to Miss Wooler's school at Mirfield, to be a teacher there,' Charlotte reminded her. 'I have an offer of a place when I am ready.'

After a long silence, Emily took up the subject again. 'I will not go,' she decided.

'Then you will displease Papa and be a burden to

him, for you must eke out a living somehow, unless a rich suitor arrives to sweep you off your feet!'

'Ha!' Casting Charlotte to one side, Emily jumped up. 'I would scorn any suitor for miles around. What would he be? A poor, stammering curate, a shy organist who plays hymns at Papa's church on Sundays?'

Charlotte too stood up, but more slowly. 'Beggars may not be choosers,' she pointed out.

'What do you mean?' Emily cried.

'Look at us – we are but poor, plain creatures.'

'Then I will not beg!' Emily decided. 'I will stay at home a spinster. Why, a walk here on the moor is worth a thousand stuttering conversations. A single breath of moorland air is enough for me to live a whole year on!'

'Unmarried and without employment – 'tis a poor prospect,' Charlotte said firmly. 'I cannot talk to you, Emily, when you are thus inclined. Your passion is too sharp a blade. It cuts me to the quick.'

'Go then. Captain and I will follow the stream to its source.' Turning on her heel and leaving Charlotte standing uncertainly by the tiny bridge, Emily strode off towards the skyline, her lean figure lit by the late afternoon sun, her green plaid skirt rustling through the heather.

She climbed regardless of the argument with Charlotte, past rows of straggling hawthorns, always on and upwards towards the windswept clouds.

'We look to the future,' Aunt Branwell confessed to a worshipper named Mrs Collins after the Sunday service.

Mr Brontë had preached on the nature of the seven deadly sins, and how each one earned the sinner an eternity in the flames of hell. 'Picture one single eternity in the burning pit,' he had warned his congregation from the tall stone pulpit in St Michael's and All Angels' Church. 'Now multiply that by seven if you can. Seven times eternity is age upon age of torment until the very end of time. Avoid the sins of lust and greed, my brethren. Think only pure thoughts, lest the wrath of our Lord God descend upon you!'

'We look to the future of my three nieces and cast around for fit employment when the time comes.' Miss Branwell saw fit to broadcast the family's plans for her charges.

'But Anne is yet young,' Mrs Collins replied. Dressed in a fine silk bonnet to match Aunt Branwell's own, and with the same front of tight curls, the parishioner took Anne's soft hand as she spoke. 'How old are you, child?'

'Twelve,' came the shy reply.

'A gentle creature to hear talk of employment,' the soft-hearted parishioner went on. 'And the prettiest of the sisters by far.'

Trembling slightly, Anne looked around Charlotte, Branwell and Emily, and saw them in a huddle inside the church porch, close to their father who spoke with members of the congregation as they left the building.

'Twelve is almost a woman,' her aunt insisted, nodding slightly at another acquaintance who passed by. 'For girls such as these a life of luxury and ease does not beckon. No, Mrs Collins, it is my duty to my poor dead sister, the girls' mother, to put them in the way of constructive work so as they do not remain a burden to their father. Something above the role of seamstress or housekeeper, as befits the station of a clergyman's daughters.'

'What do you have in mind?' Mrs Collins asked, still squeezing Anne's trembling hand. She was tall and upright, wearing a dainty cameo on a ribbon around her throat, with good lace on her cuffs and fine, white kid gloves.

'My brother-in-law wishes them to go as governesses or teachers,' Aunt Branwell told her. 'Charlotte may go to Miss Wooler at Mirfield if she pleases.'

Anne quaked. She had heard Emily talk defiantly of staying at home and not putting herself up before strangers. And she knew that, contrariwise, Charlotte was already resigned to such a course. At twelve, she had thought herself far too young to make the choice herself.

'Better to go out as a governess to a good family,' was

Mrs Collins's opinion. 'The hours of work may be long and the payment small, but such a place is respectable, and with a kind mistress all may be well.'

Aunt Branwell nodded sharply. 'Charlotte is almost of an age to do such a thing. She talks of learning French before taking the position at Mirfield, but my opinion is that she merely procrastinates.'

'You truly wish to find a position for Charlotte?' Mrs Collins repeated thoughtfully.

Anne shook in her shoes. A position for Charlotte. A breaking-up of the family! Who then would make the bedtime plays with Branwell and breathe life into the world of Angria?

'Yes, Mrs Collins – Mr Brontë would be grateful for news of any family wanting a governess at present,' Aunt insisted. An unsmiling, reserved woman, she ignored Anne's pleading looks.

The parishioner cast around in her mind. 'My neighbour, Mrs Williams, is in want of a teacher for her twin sons. They are six years old.'

'Boys would not do for Charlotte in her first position,' Aunt decided.

'And there is a family I know of at Hartcross,' Mrs Collins murmured uncertainly. 'Mr and Mrs Holmes, with a daughter and a son. They have lately lost a governess and would take another who came well recommended.'

'What age is the daughter?' Aunt inquired.

'Ah, she is not a little girl. Above twelve years, although I forget exactly.'

'Too old,' Aunt said. 'Charlotte would not fare well in such a situation unless the children be little and impressionable.'

The kindly woman concurred.

And so the subject was dropped for the time being, and the summer turned into autumn without change.

Three

The hawk tore at the meat between Emily's forefinger and thumb. She felt the thud of its beak through her strong leather glove.

How does the world seem from high in the sky? she wondered. *How does it feel to soar?* Creamy white sinews in the meat stretched and snapped. The bird tipped back its head and swallowed a tasty red morsel. When he had finished, Emily kept him carefully at arm's length and returned him to the stone wash-room at the bottom of the yard. He hopped onto his perch and regarded her with a baleful eye.

'I shall call you Hero,' she decided.

'There is a weakness in your father's lungs.' Aunt Branwell had gathered the three girls into her upstairs room to remind them of the their pressing situation. 'It is an illness which almost took his life two summers since, and which may still return.'

'Papa will not die!' Anne whispered.

Aunt regarded her sternly. 'We must all die, child.'

Emily and Charlotte stood to either side of Anne, their faces expressionless, their figures upright, like sentinels.

'If your papa were indeed to depart this life, his successor would take both his living and this house. I have an income of a mere fifty pounds per year, and so could not afford to keep you.'

'We understand that, Aunt, and are grateful for your concern.' Charlotte spoke up as she always did. 'We will take good care of Papa's health, and pray to God to keep him.'

Their aunt bowed her head realising that her nieces must think her severe. She knew that she lacked her sister Maria's softer nature. 'Forgive me for speaking too plainly,' she murmured. And for not always acting as your mama would have wished.'

'No, Aunt.' Charlotte's gaze was steady. 'You have been a mother to us more than many another would. You have raised us according to your beliefs.'

This brought a smile to the older woman's thin lips. 'I feel how it is to stand condemned with faint praise,' she acknowledged. 'But bless you, Charlotte, for an honest reply!'

Emily regarded her aunt with the kind of interest a deer would give a hunter – wary, ever alert to danger. 'You wish to tell us something in particular?' she asked quietly.

'In particular, no,' Aunt Branwell confessed. 'In general, we must be certain between ourselves that your way is the way of duty, and we must not expect these pleasant habits of childhood to continue beyond another year or two at most.'

Anne sighed and hung her head.

'What of Branwell, Aunt?' Emily challenged. 'Is he to follow the way of duty also?'

Her aunt stiffened. 'The case for your brother is different. His future lies in the hands of your papa, who dreams of an artist's life for his only son.'

'Not duty, then.'

Charlotte glanced sideways as Emily delivered this last abrupt remark. 'Branwell has great gifts,' she reminded her. 'Papa believes in him and wishes to nurture those talents. We must not resent it.'

'Ah but you do, Charlotte!' Emily cried, forgetting the restraints imposed by Aunt Branwell's presence. 'I have heard you say that you wished it was you who was to go to London in his place. Deny it if you can!'

Charlotte closed her eyes as if to compose herself. 'It was weakness that made me confess as much,' she insisted. That weakness is called jealousy, and it is a deadly sin which I must fight against with all my might!'

Emily saw her sister's distress and was sorry to have caused it. However, she turned her continuing anger on her guardian. 'One or two years at most, Aunt? And then the prison door of duty closes in on us – even on Anne, else you would not have brought her to your room.'

'Do not look at me in that way, Emily, with that savage air of defiance.'

Emily looked as she would at a jailer wearing the keys that would lock her prison door. *I will set my hawk, Hero, free*, she thought. But she said nothing more to her aunt, and instead lowered her gaze to the patterned carpet on the floor.

'Go down and help Tabby with the dinner,' a defeated Aunt Branwell said in the lull.

The girls turned and went from the room, past the tall clock on the stairs, through the hall and the dining room into the kitchen at the back of the house.

'What is the matter with you, Emily?' Branwell asked brazenly at dinner. He had been to Halifax for his lesson in painting and had returned in the village cart. There were blue and yellow stains on his fingers and a devil-may-care look in his eye.

'Nothing that you can remedy, Bany,' Emily replied. She toyed with her food and longed for the meal to be ended. 'I have been thinking that I will set Hero free tonight,' she declared, looking up from her plate and across the table into Charlotte's troubled eyes. 'His broken wing is mended and so I have decided – I will return him to the moor from whence he came.'

Four

Emily went alone, except for Captain and the wild bird which she intended to set free. The setting sun cast long shadows and was still warm on her back when she placed the cedar box lined with lambs' fleece on the ground and opened the lid.

Inside, her hand felt the soft warmth of the hawk's breast. Its tiny, rapid heartbeat made her own heart beat more quickly, then, remembering the leather glove which she carried at her waist, she swiftly withdrew her hand and slipped it into the protective casing.

'Stay back, Captain,' she warned, as the dog nuzzled up to the box.

Captain whined and withdrew to a safe distance.

'Now, Hero!' Emily murmured, waiting for the hawk to emerge.

She saw his round, shining eye, fierce beak and speckled, beating breast. Surprised that he did not move, she offered her gloved hand and watched him raise himself and step onto her cupped hand.

'There,' she whispered, lifting him free of the box.

Hero blinked. The eyelid came down like a shutter, then flicked up. He ducked his head and pecked softly at the glove.

'There's no meat. I don't mean to feed you, my bonny bird, I mean to set you free.'

Another flick of the eyelid, then a slight lifting of his wings told her that he grew ready to fly.

'The sky is yours,' she promised. 'And all this earth below. Go now.'

Hero spread his wings then let them drop. His cruel claws still gripped her gloved hand. To one side, Captain let a low growl rumble in his throat.

Emily stood straight and held her arm wide and straight. She raised Hero towards the horizon, offering him liberty.

He took it at last, spreading his wings, and with a flap, ascending into thin air, gradually beating with an ever stronger rhythm, rising away from her, beginning to fly. Emily's heart soared with him.

She watched him rise and catch an air current, wheel into the wind, so that a gust of air carried him and his wings ceased to beat. He rode the east wind, effortless, beautiful.

'Come, Captain,' Emily said abruptly, picking up the box and turning down the hill.

But the dog stayed, crouched in the heather, chin to the ground, still growling.

'Come!' she commanded. The sun, which had turned the western sky a flaming red, was even now sinking behind the hill. She must walk quickly to reach home before night fell.

Captain did not respond, however. His hackles had risen and he stood, legs full square, his top lip curled back and his white teeth gleaming in his black muzzle.

Emily frowned and looked around. Had the dog seen or heard something close by of which she was unaware? She looked again, only partly familiar with this spot close to the brow of the steep hill which overlooked a wild, uninhabited valley beyond. On this side of the ridge, there were scattered cottages and sheep-folds and low stone walls criss-crossing the slopes – all signs of man's presence.

'What is it?' she said to Captain, watching him with interest as he turned and bounded several steps towards the ridge.

He had made towards a gap in one of the black, moss-covered walls, and now waited for her to follow. The gap was edged by tall stone posts, designed to be narrow at the foot but wider at the top, so that a man might pass through but a beast might not.

'If this is but a rabbit or pheasant, I shall be angered,' Emily warned Captain. 'Aunt will chide us if we're late home.'

The dog waited stubbornly by the gap until she ordered him on. Understanding what a sheep did not – that he might leap high and so pass through the barrier, Captain hurtled through the gap then ran on towards a mean, abandoned building on the brow of the hill.

Emily knew the old shepherd's cot She had passed it by on many a lonely walk – always by herself, or with her beloved dog, since this spot was higher and more remote than either Charlotte or Anne was willing to come. Long abandoned, most of the roof was gone and the timbers were falling into the stone shell. The door hung off its hinges, the stone-flagged approach was choked with weeds.

She knew it well, but at this moment felt reluctant to approach. Why had Captain led her here, and why had she followed when reason told her to turn for home before the sun finally set? What was there about the place that seemed somehow different?

Emily stood, watched and listened.

Water tumbled between the banks of a nearby stream, falling over rocks and splashing into deep, clear pools. The sound distracted her, so that for a moment she took her eyes off Captain growling at the locked gate.

The growl rose to a snarl, and within a moment her dog was locked in combat with a second creature – bigger and bulkier than her swift Captain – brown in colour, and with jaws that locked themselves around the enemy's neck.

With a cry Emily sprang forward. The brown dog had drawn blood and she thought only to separate them.

So she came between them, wrenching at the enemy's head to twist him away, finding that she wasn't strong enough, feeling the dog's breath on her arm as his teeth snapped. Then the two dogs rolled away through the heather, still locked in combat, and she looked down at her hand to see that it too bled from a gash across her palm.

'Damn you, who taught you to come between two dogs?' an angry voice demanded.

Emily's head whirled, the dogs snarled and fought. She thought she saw a figure hovering over her as she sank to the ground.

'By God, she faints!' the voice complained, as a man's face came close, a lock of dark hair falling across his brow, the deepset eyes staring into hers.

She came to in the cool shade cast by the cottage wall. Captain lay at her side, still panting and bleeding from the mouth, while his powerful enemy strained at a thick rope staked deep into the ground. Of Emily's surly rescuer there was nothing to be seen. She soon found however that he must have acted on her behalf. Besides tethering the savage dog, he had bound the tear in the flesh of her palm with a clean strip of coarse, cotton cloth such as would make a plain working-man's shirt. It seemed too that he had gone to the stream, dipped more of the same fabric in the cool, clear water and returned to lay it across her brow. Now it had slipped and lay on the stone flags.

She raised herself onto her elbows, calling for Captain and feeling deep relief when she saw him only a little the worse for his experience, with a small wound in his lower jaw. He had bled profusely, but suffered no lasting harm.

Emily frowned as she tried to stand. Her own wound throbbed and her head still whirled. But she would raise herself and look around, seeking to know more.

'Who is there?' she called.

Captain licked his wound and gave a low whine. There was no reply.

'If you are hiding, show yourself!'

Again, nothing, except the thickset brown dog straining at his tether. Evidently her rescuer was not only surly in manner, but also reluctant to accept her thanks. She recalled his fierce greeting and the intense look in his dark eyes as he'd stooped over her.

'Very well, I will say my thanks and leave you to your ruined cottage!' Emily spoke boldly, called Captain to heel and set off across the yard. 'Should you seek a reward, my name is Emily Jane Brontë, and my papa is vicar of St Michael's at Haworth!'

The words were scarcely out before faintness overcame her a second time and she sank to the ground.

'I know who you are!' The same figure as before appeared, this time from within the shell of the house. The man strode to support her before she swooned away. 'What need do I have of a reward?' he scorned. 'Unless your father's brand of religion extends to the granting of impossible wishes, like the wizard in an old tale!'

Emily's eyelids flickered shut then opened again. A second glance told her that her rescuer was more a youth than a man – scarcely past eighteen or nineteen years of age, with thick, unruly black hair, and truly gypsy-like in his countenance. For the first time it struck her that she ought to be afraid.

'Will you stand?' he demanded, drawing her roughly to her feet and thrusting Captain to one side. 'What foolishness draws you onto the moor at nightfall, damn you?'

Emily gasped as the youth cursed her a second time.

'I say, stand!' Setting her back on her feet, he picked up the wet rag and thrust it against her forehead. 'Perhaps this will revive you. Now go before I release the dog to do his work!'

Using all her willpower to steady herself, Emily broke free of his rough grasp. 'Better you had left me to swoon than curse me so!' she declared angrily. 'Why did you step in?'

'Because the dog is a brute with sharp teeth and strong jaws. He would have killed yours and then started on you, had I not laid into him with a heavy stick.' The youth watched her warily, looking now as if he regretted that he had not left the dog to do its worst.

'Then I do thank you, for Captain's sake,' she said more calmly. Her head was beginning to clear, her legs felt stronger. 'I had no idea that the cottage was inhabited, else I should never have stepped into the yard.'

A humourless smile came onto the stranger's face. The cottage is not *inhabited*, as you call it. I was merely passing by.'

'You are far from home, then?' She thought she knew the face of every soul in Haworth.

The smile turned into a contemptuous sneer. The youth took up the thick stick he had mentioned and whipped it across the feathery heads of some long grass that had turned to seed. 'Practise your Sunday school manners on those more fitting to receive them. They are wasted on me.'

This last rebuff sent her marching for the gate. She

tugged hard at the iron latch, but found it rusted and jammed.

'You must climb over,' came the taunting advice. 'Your cowardly dog may slide between the bars.'

No sooner said than she gathered her skirts and began to scale the gate with as much dignity as she could muster. In spite of her throbbing, bloody hand, she made short work of it and began to stride down the rough hillside.

'Wait!' the youth commanded. 'I have a favour to ask.'

Emily turned to see him lounging against the gate, the silhouette of the ruined cottage behind him, the golden red sky fading to dove-grey overhead.

'You wish to thank and reward me?' he reminded her.

A brief nod confirmed this, but she stood on her guard. What strange request was he about to make?

'You will oblige me by telling no one about this meeting,' he said in a voice used by a master towards his servant. And yet he was dressed almost as a beggar, in an open-necked shirt and waistcoat roughly made from a sheep's skin.

'What do you mean?'

'I wish for it to be kept secret.'

'Secret' was said with a hissing, close sound, through clenched teeth.

Emily held up her wounded hand. 'Then I must say that I was attacked by spirits or phantoms, not by living beings.'

'Say what you will, only do not mention me,' he repeated. 'This is how you will show your gratitude.'

She nodded slowly.

'A promise, then?'

'Yes,' she agreed, then turned and walked on.

The sky was almost dark when Emily reached the parsonage. She entered by the back door. Tabby flew out of the kitchen with a cry when she saw her bloodied hand.

'The hawk tore at it when I set him free,' Emily said quietly, unable to meet the servant's gaze. 'Tell Aunt and Papa that I am home.'

Five

'Emily is forbidden from taking her walks,' Branwell reported to Charlotte early the next day. 'I have heard Papa agree with Aunt that she should be confined to her room for a whole week.'

Anne stirred a pot of oatmeal which simmered on the stove. 'Emily will never endure it,' she murmured.

Charlotte cut through one of Tabby's crusty loaves with a sharp knife. Outwardly at least, she sided with the adults over the latest Emily affair. 'Yes and maybe she will take care in future not to run about the moors at nightfall, if the punishment is to be locked up in the house thereafter.'

'I doubt it,' Branwell commented, seizing a slice of the bread. He chewed for a while, then went on, 'Emily says that the hawk pecked at her hand, but I don't believe her!'

'Why would she lie?' Charlotte demanded.

Her brother shrugged, sniffing at the porridge and pulling a face. 'Give that to the pigs!' he told Anne, who frowned and stirred more vigorously.

'Emily doesn't lie as a rule,' he admitted. 'But there is something suspicious about this tale she tells. Did you see her downcast look, and how she avoided speaking directly with Papa? And who gave her the bandage to bind her hand – did none of you ask her that?'

Just then there was a noise at the door and Emily herself appeared. Her face was pale and angry-looking, her naturally wavy brown hair pulled severely back. 'Ask her now!' she challenged Branwell. 'Since she is here, you may accuse her of lying to her face, instead of behind her back!'

A moment later Tabby swept in from the scullery and broke the dark mood. 'Pour out the porridge, Anne,' she ordered. 'And Charlotte, spread butter on that bread and take a piece to your papa in the parlour. He is busy there with his sermon.'

And so the argument was avoided. After breakfast, Emily retired with a copy of *Gulliver's Travels* to the small bedroom at the top of the landing, refusing to answer Charlotte's questions about the previous night, saying only that she could not bear to be doubted and put on the spot by Branwell, whose word could never be trusted on any subject whatsoever.

It was only after Branwell had set out for Halifax and Charlotte and Anne had settled in the drawing room for an afternoon's sewing that Emily emerged again into the kitchen, where Tabby was at work.

'Let me prick out the pastry for the pies,' she offered, making herself useful in spite of her injured hand.

Tabby saw she meant to make up for her recent misbehaviour. 'You may think it easy to please me,' she grumbled as she rolled and shaped. 'But you will have more to do than prick pastry to get back in your aunt's good books.'

'Don't chide, Tabby. I am not a child – I may go out of the house when I please, though Aunt thinks otherwise.' Emily waited until Tabby had laid the pastry into its tins before she took a fork and marked the tops.

'Your aunt thinks of your reputation. A clergyman's daughter should not play the gypsy by roaming the moor at sunset.'

'A clergyman's daughter must not do this . . . do that . . . be this . . . be that!' With each mocking phrase, Emily lightly pricked the pastry cases. Then she changed the subject of their conversation as casually as she could. 'Tabby, what do you know of the shepherds' cots up there on the moor top? Are many still inhabited?'

Tabby wiped her floury hands on her apron. 'Which cottages do you mean? The ones by Timble Crag, or to the west by Haygarth Falls?'

'Up by the falls. I was there last night, setting Hero

free. So many of the old houses seem to be falling into ruins.'

'Aye well, those who farmed those high hills are all gone to the hollows to work in the mills,' Tabby told her. 'That has happened in my lifetime, for when I was a girl those cottages were warm and tight, not letting in the rain as they do now. It's a sorry sight, they say, though I haven't walked those hills myself in many a year. They say too that the walls that mark out the hillsides are broken and mouldering back into the sod, that the sheep come up from the valleys in summer and roam where they will.'

'Yes, but even so, do you know of any that are still occupied?' Emily insisted.

With a final clap of her hands to dismiss the floury coating, Tabby shook her head. 'Nay, the only occupants of the moor top are the fairies who flit through the night, doing their mischief. All sane and sensible folk keep to the valleys, out of the wind and frost.'

'Hmm.' Emily nodded and said no more. Later that evening she sought out her father and read to him from Milton's *Paradise Lost*. By bedtime she had secured his promise that she should be released early from her confinement in the house.

'Tomorrow, Papa!' she'd pleaded. 'I shall die unless I am permitted outside!'

'You will not die from staying indoors, Emily,' her father contradicted flatly. But he laid his hand on her head and stroked her hair. 'You are like a caged bird, are you not?'

She looked directly into his eyes. 'I love to wander, Papa. It is September, and soon the nights will close in. The winter will be long enough.'

He nodded and sighed. 'I will speak with your Aunt Branwell,' he agreed.

'Emily has wheedled herself back into Papa's good books,' Branwell the eavesdropper reported back to Charlotte and Anne. 'Aunt is defeated. Emily is free.'

Six

In late September of 1832, a week after Emily had been released from her imprisonment, a stranger approached the front door of the parsonage. He was small and rounded in appearance, with a balding head and long ginger side whiskers curling about his cheeks.

'I wish to speak with the Reverend Patrick Brontë,' he announced to Tabby in a self-important voice. 'Please tell him that Mr William Whitehouse awaits his convenience.'

'Master's from home,' Tabby replied, recognising at once the name of Branwell's Halifax tutor. She glanced over her shoulder to see Aunt Branwell descending the narrow stairs. 'You must speak to his sister,' she told the visitor uneasily.

'Mr Whitehouse, please come into the parlour,' the children's aunt said in her usual cool tone. 'We were not expecting visitors, as you see.'

Inside the best room of the house, Charlotte and Anne were sewing while Emily worked at a pencil sketch of Captain, who lay quietly at her feet. Branwell was nowhere to be seen.

'Excuse me, but the matter is delicate,' Whitehouse said with an exaggeratedly embarrassed stutter, clearing his throat and indicating with his eyes that Aunt Branwell might prefer to clear the young people from the room.

But she kept her head up and her gaze frank. 'We have no secrets in this house, Mr Whitehouse. You may speak up.'

The artist wrung his hands together nervously. 'Very well,' he went on. 'It is regarding the payment of certain fees – money due to me for the tuition I provide for your nephew, Branwell Brontë, in my studio in Halifax . . .'

Aunt Branwell let the man stammer to a halt, then took up the reins. 'Yes, yes, I am aware of the nature of the payment, Mr Whitehouse. Branwell comes to you on a weekly basis for the sum of two shillings and sixpence per lesson. He has been attending since the early part of August. I provide my nephew with the exact amount on each occasion. By my reckoning that comes to a total of one pound five shillings. What of it?'

'Madam, that's entirely my point. I mean, the sum of one pound five shillings. It is not a king's ransome, I admit . . . However . . .'

Once more the visitor's confidence gave out and he was reduced to silence.

It was up to Charlotte to enlighten her elderly relative. 'I think Mr Whitehouse means to tell you, Aunt, that he has not thus far received the money due to him,' she explained, drawing herself up with all the dignity she could muster in her slight, seventeen-year-old frame.

'Quite so!' the artist agreed breathlessly. 'Madam, I had hoped to discuss this matter face to face with Mr Brontë, for he has declined to answer the letters sent by me via his son's hand.'

'You have sent my brother reminders through Branwell?' Aunt Branwell queried. 'How can this be? What has happened to the money? Surely Branwell has handed you a sealed envelope containing the payment at the end of each lesson?'

'Exactly my point – I mean to say – no, Madam, he has not!'

As Emily, Charlotte and Anne's faces betrayed their distress, Aunt Branwell's merely grew more pointed and sharp. 'No money at all?' she insisted.

'Not a penny.' Despite his embarrassment, the artist was adamant. 'The case looks serious, does it not? If I am to understand you, your nephew has been dishonest . . .'

Once more Aunt Branwell silenced him with a glance.

'Thank you, Mr Whitehouse. I will speak with Branwell. He is from home with his father at present.'

Her frosty tone seemed to incite the uneasy visitor. 'I hope you are not doubting my word,' he said angrily.

'No, Sir. But before I can proceed, I must speak at length with my brother and my nephew.'

'And leave me without payment?'

'For the present, until I have heard my nephew's account of events, it is best to let the matter rest,' Aunt Branwell insisted.

But Whitehouse had travelled a long way in uncomfortable heat and was not about to depart without having his full say. 'You will also notify your brother that I no longer wish to tutor his son in the skills of portraiture and landscape painting.'

'I will,' Aunt Branwell said frostily.

'Putting aside the matter of payment,' the artist rushed on unguardedly, 'there is the fact that my pupil does not prove himself apt or willing. In fact, I venture to say that were he to display all the willingness in the world, his talent would not amount to a scrap. No, Madam – Branwell does not display one single ounce of talent as a painter!'

At this Emily stood up to defend her brother, 'Mr Whitehouse,' she said angrily. 'My aunt has told you that she will talk with Papa. It is the most she can promise in the unfortunate circumstance. She does not wish to hear her nephew's name further dragged through the mud.'

Whitehouse laughed at the interruption. Then he turned back to Aunt Branwell. 'Very well, in front of these tender witnesses, as you would have it yourself, Madam, I demand full payment of my account and declare my intention to cease forthwith all further contact with your brother and his family.'

With this, and without further ceremony, he turned and went.

It was if a stone had been dropped into a deep, still pond. Ripples began at the centre and moved outwards in clear, concentric circles, affecting every aspect of life at the parsonage for weeks to come.

Aunt Branwell did her duty of reporting Branwell's dishonesty to her brother, then withdrew. It was up to the boy's father to discipline him and decide upon the punishment.

'Poor Aunt,' Anne said, unable to say clearly why her sympathy had attached itself there, except that it was Aunt Branwell's money that had been lost.

'Poor Papa!' Charlotte cried. Their father's hopes were dashed, disappointment showed in his bowed head and preoccupied air.

'And poor Branwell,' Emily said to the birds and the beasts as she walked near Timble Crag. No one knew how he had spent the stolen money – only that Branwell bore Whitehouse's criticism of his artistic ability very ill. 'What is he to do if he is not to be a great artist?' she continued. 'He will not stomach the life of an office clerk, ruling lines in a ledger and writing lists!'

Branwell himself had first complained that Mr Whitehouse was a bad teacher who did not inspire his pupil. 'He would have me measure and study perspective, he grumbled. 'But as to letting me lay brush to canvas, there was little enough of that!' Besides, the bald little man was vain and pompous, forever recalling his glory days at the Royal College in London.

Then, when this whining had increased his father's displeasure, Branwell had turned defiant. 'I care not for Papa's disappointed looks!' he'd declared to the three girls. 'I can bear a sour look as well as the next man.'

Emily, Charlotte and Anne had shrunk into themselves. They understood heroics and romance in the works of Sir Walter Scott and the great Lord Byron, not this home-grown pettiness and self deceit.

Branwell's weakness disturbed Emily the most. She would escape to the moor and sigh over her brother, on another occasion finding herself once again up at Timble Crag and striding east along the ridge towards Haygarth Fall. Almost before she knew it, she was upon the ruined cottage – the scene of Captain's encounter with the savage dog.

Curiosity held her as she stood at the barred gate. She wondered again about the dark haired youth and the solemn promise which she'd made and kept. Where had he come from and whither had he gone? For today, at noon, with a rich autumn smell of heather and fern in the air, there was no one to be seen as she stared across the yard at the house.

She would have moved on, except that a noise from the far corner of the yard drew her – the sound of an animal whimpering, perhaps in pain.

Emily's heart jumped. She climbed the gate and approached a mossy stone trough whose stagnant surface was covered in green slime. It was from beyond the trough that the sound had seemed to come.

There was a further whine as she pushed aside nettles and peered into the damp, dark corner, and saw with another sharp shock that a dog lay on its side, chained to a rusting iron ring in the wall. It seemed too weak to stand and move away.

At first she didn't recognise the creature as the same one that had savaged her own dear Captain. Its brown coat was covered in dirt, its ribcage heaving up and down in an effort to breathe. The glazed look in its eye told her that it was close to death.

Emily gasped as the dog struggled to lift its head. 'You're starved!' she cried, straight away skimming the slime off the trough and scooping up a handful of brown water to offer to the dog's lips. The water trickled to the ground as the sufferer turned its head away. 'What devil has done this?'

Springing to her feet, she looked around. She must find food and comfort for the suffering beast, so she ran quickly to the bare, rotting door of the cottage, pushed at it and felt it give way. Stepping inside, she looked up at the fallen roof and the heavy timbers still precariously in place. It was dangerous to proceed, and yet she might find something in here – an implement of some sort – that would help unchain the dog.

Lifting the hem of her skirt, she climbed over a pile of rubble and entered a small room to one side of the doorway, where part of the roof was still intact. She made out a fireplace, and to her surprise a blackened kettle standing in the ashes of what seemed to be a recent fire. There was also an oak settle to one side of the fire, with a blanket of rough sacking on it, and beside the settle a few oddments of kitchen utensils – a pewter platter bent out of shape, a cracked pot mug, and best of all a knife with a blade that was still clean and sharp.

Emily seized the knife and ran outside. The dog's whining had ceased as she fell onto her knees and began to hack with the blade at the thick rope around its neck. If she could cut through the rope, she could slide the dog free of the chain.

She worked hard, chafing with the knife and feeling the hessian cords snap one by one. But the dog lay without responding, its breathing shallow, its eyes gradually closing, even though rescue was so close at hand.

'Who has done this!' Emily repeated, breaking through the rope at last and lifting the chain away. Once more she tried to trickle water into the dog's mouth. She stroked his head and brushed the thick dust from it.

His eyes were closed. The rise and fall of the ribcage lessened. He breathed his last.

Emily dropped the knife and let her head sink onto her chest. She overlooked the dog's previous savagery and cursed its cruel owner. 'No beast should suffer what you have suffered,' she murmured, standing up and vowing that, at whatever cost, she would call his owner to account.

'Emily grows apace. She looks in good health,' Mrs Collins remarked.

It was the day after Emily's most recent visit to Haygarth Falls.

'She is the tallest of the girls,' Aunt Branwell conceded.

'And the least contented,' the neighbour surmised, watching Emily struggle to teach the letters of the alphabet to a mill child whose mother had seen fit, on the first sabbath in October, to send him unwashed and ill-clad to Sunday school. Emily, dressed in Sunday best of grey, figured silk, strove to be patient, but she sighed and tapped the chalk against the slate, watching the boy fumble.

'Oh no, Emily is easily pleased,' Aunt contradicted. 'She is a simple soul – happy with her lot, so long as she has the freedom to roam. Anne too is content. It is only Charlotte who rails against her destiny.'

Mrs Collins seemed unconvinced, but the two women continued to survey the busy scene in the church porch, where six or seven ragged pupils scratched at their slates and the three Brontë girls bent over them.

'Do you make progress with your plans for Charlotte?' Mrs Collins inquired. Her interest was kindly, since she lacked daughters of her own and had thoughts to spare on behalf of others.

Aunt Branwell shook her head. 'My brother's attention is all on my nephew at present,' was all she would say.

'Then I must insist that you speak with my acquaintance, Mrs Holmes of Hartcross, of whom I talked. I hear through her that there are several families of that parish who look about themselves for a governess. Mrs Holmes is acquainted with them all.'

And so it was arranged for Mrs Holmes of Hartcross

to take tea with Aunt Branwell at the parsonage. Her children, Martha and James, accompanied her, stepping out of a smart carriage with their mama and staring with open distaste at the plainly dressed, serious and subdued Brontë girls.

'Emily, take Martha for a walk through the village,' Aunt Branwell instructed, choosing her because she was closest in age to the visitor. 'Charlotte, you must find Branwell. James too would like a companion, I'm sure.'

So saying, she led Mrs Holmes through the door.

'Your name is Emily?' Martha Holmes inquired to break the long silence.

The two girls passed down a steep cobbled street by the Black Bull Inn at the head of Haworth's Main Street. Emily felt awkward and dull beside the splendidly dressed guest. She nodded, stepping to one side as the cart carrying mail and sacks of flour struggled up the hill. The grey pony between the traces pulled steadily, the cart rattled and swayed.

'My name is Martha. I am soon to go to school in Brussels, at the Pensionnat Seurat on the Rue d'Isabelle.'

Emily saw that the proposed plan, glamorous as it sounded, did not please the girl, but her own reticence prevented her from taking up the conversation. She caught sight of a reflection of the two of them in the apothecary's window – one small and slender, with shining fair ringlets, dressed in a fine straw bonnet and light dress of green-sprigged muslin, the other bare-headed and dressed in her frock of workaday plaid.

'It is Papa's idea,' Martha Holmes said with a frown. 'He thinks to take me away from . . . from Hartcross, and from . . . well, never mind from whom!'

The bad tempered half-confession from a stranger unnerved Emily, whose own nature was intensely private. She would never discuss family affairs in this way.

'Have you ever been in love?' Martha asked with a sigh, apropos of nothing.

Emily shook her head.

'I have. I am still. My father thinks to put a distance between me and my *amour*, but my heart is constant. I shall not fall out of love simply because the sea separates us, shall I?'

Another shake of the head and a quizzical look from Emily. Was this how the romance of Walter Scott played out in real life – with a shallow, over-familiar ringleted girl frowning and stamping her white-stockinged, daintily-shod foot on the cobbles of Haworth's Main Street?

'There is Branwell!' Emily said suddenly, and with relief, spying her brother and James Holmes coming towards them through the churchyard.

'Such goings on at Hartcross Manor!' Sally Mosley reported to Tabby over the steaming tub in the washhouse the following Monday morning. Tabby's helper had heard of Mrs Holmes's visit and was bursting with gossip. 'They say that the trouble has quite undermined the father and that he keeps to his bed. The doctor says he may not last the winter.'

'Tut.' Tabby sniffed and clicked her tongue. 'All I know is that Mrs Holmes has recommended two respectable families in search of a governess to Miss Branwell. That is neighbourly work, and good of the lady to make the effort.'

'Did you see the daughter?' Sally went on unabashed. 'Her dress was so fine, and her bonnet was all decked out with ribbon! Emily looked a moth beside the butterfly when they walked down the street together!'

'Hush!' was Tabby's reply. She thumped at the laundry with her three-pronged pole. It was likely that Emily or one of the other girls might be listening from the yard. 'They're hanging out the bed linen, so mind your tongue.'

'Aye but the Holmes's story is all around the valley where they live! There's talk of nothing else from Hartcross right down to Halifax!' Surrounded by steam, with her sleeves rolled back, young Sally was in her element. 'Tabby, leave off your tutting and your shushing – this is as good a tale as ever came out of these hollows!'

'And all the better for not being repeated,' Tabby said primly.

'Well, for my part, if I were the young lady in question, I'd run off with the lad and have done with it!' Sally declared, driven on by the realisation that Emily and Anne had finished the pegging out of the washing and were indeed standing listening near to the wash-house door. 'Once done, a deed like that cannot be undone, and it would be a hard-hearted father who kept the girl out of his will in the long run!'

'What lad? What young lady?' Anne poked her head into the steaming room and asked to share in the idle chatter. 'Are we talking of elopement? Oh Sally, tell us!'

Sally grinned broadly at Tabby. 'Listen, Anne! You recall Martha Holmes, who was here last week? She only went and fell head over heels in love with her papa's groom! They say he secretly courted the girl and turned her head with flattery, and she, being young, fell for it. The two were about to elope together on Mr Holmes's best stallion, when the son, James, discovered it.'

Anne's eyes gleamed, while Emily, who still stood outside the door, listened intently. She thought with scorn of Martha Holmes's high voice as she swore that she should not fall out of love merely because the sea separated her from her 'amour'.

'Hush. It's a poor, common story!' Tabby protested. ' 'Tis a pity that a young girl's head can so easily be turned, is it not, Emily?'

'But what happened to the lovers?' Anne insisted. 'When the brother discovered them, what happened then?'

'Mr Holmes dismissed the ungrateful lad, though he had taken him in at first as an orphan and lavished the care of a father upon him. They say the daughter is to go to school in foreign parts,' Sally reported.

'That's true,' Emily said curtly.

'And the groom?' Anne asked. 'What of him?'

Sally emerged into the daylight, her wrists and hands red with washing, strands of lank brown hair sticking to her hot face. 'No one knows!' she declared. 'He disappeared, but first he swore revenge against the brother, who betrayed him.'

'And is he likely to exact his revenge? Where is he now? What does he do? How does he look?'

Sally laughed out loud at Anne's eagerness. 'It's a mystery!' she declared. 'The lad left Hartcross in disgrace. No one knows what became of him.'

Anne sighed and clasped her hands, while Tabby brushed by with a fresh basket of washed linen. 'Peg these to the line!' she instructed Anne sternly.

But Sally couldn't resist adding a fanciful ending to her tale of the star-crossed lovers. 'Why,' she said, 'for all we know, the poor lad could be dead of a broken heart and lying on the moor top, his body mouldering back into the earth!'

Emily Jane Bronte's Diary paper, October 1832

It is Friday evening, near eight o'clock – wild, rainy weather. I am seated in the dining room alone, having just concluded writing chapter XIII of *The Gondalians* with Anne. All the princes and princesses are at the Palace of Instruction, excepting Henry Angora, Juliet Angusteena and Julian Egremont who are in exile.

Aunt is in the parlour reading *Blackwood's Magazine* to Papa. We are all stout and hearty, though not without agitation over the failure of the scheme to turn Branwell into an artist. Papa says we must try again when the time comes.

I am contemplating a further visit to Haygarth Falls before the winter sets in. My mind runs on the cruel death of the poor beast and on the monster who left him to starve.

Aunt: *Come, Emily, it's past eight o'clock*

Emily: *Yes Aunt*

Anne: *Well, shall we write the next chapter this evening?*

Emily: *What do you think?*

We agreed to go upstairs first to make sure if we got into the humour. However, we may go to sleep instead.

Seven

'A recommendation from Mrs Holmes of Hartcross cannot come untainted by the unfortunate circumstance in which that family finds itself!' Papa declared when he heard from Aunt Branwell of their distant neighbour's visit.

'What do you mean, brother?' Aunt stood on her dignity against the pompous criticism.

'I mean that family trouble oftentimes colours the judgment. Those persons recommended by poor Mrs Holmes would require independent investigation before we were to consider them as suitable employers for Charlotte.'

A pained expression came into Aunt Branwell's eyes, half hidden in the flickering lamp-light of the parlour. She began to suspect that her brother was not committed to their agreed course of sending Charlotte out as a governess.

The girls sewed, Branwell wrote the frontispiece to the latest Glasstown saga – 'Letters from an Englishman to his Friend in London by Captain John Flower,

Volume IV, October 10th AD 1832'. His hand was cramped but neat on the tiny page.

'Am I to understand that you do not extend the hand of Christian charity as far as our neighbours in Hartcross?' Aunt asked drily.

Mr Brontë ignored the sarcasm. 'I merely remark that the judgment of poor Mrs Holmes may not be entirely sound.'

Anne looked up from her work at Emily, hoping to catch her eye. By 'family trouble', surely Papa must mean the fascinating story of the groom's near elopement with Martha Holmes. Perhaps now they would hear more of the tragic affair.

Emily kept her head down and stitched doggedly. An unclear suspicion that the stranger at the Falls was one and the same as the disgraced groom at Hartcross Manor had grown into a near certainty in her mind.

'The lady's judgment seemed sound to me,' Aunt Branwell sniffed. 'I see you do not intend to pursue the recommendation, however.'

Mr Brontë nodded curtly. 'Quite so. I would prefer no further intercourse between my girls and Martha Holmes,' he said with firm finality.

So Charlotte breathed again. Her fingers pulled the needle swiftly to and fro. She was not to go as a governess – not yet.

'Stand! What secrets do you know?' Branwell challenged Emily. 'The Genii Brannii demands to be told!'

Emily sighed and tried to push her brother to one side. He stood between her and her walk onto the moor on the occasion she'd chosen to return once more to the cottage at Haygarth Falls. 'I don't know what you mean,' she said crossly. 'Stand aside, Bany or I shall set Captain on you!'

'Ha!' he swaggered. 'That cur cannot harm the brave Rogue, black sheep of the noble Percy family – bright with beauty, dark with crime!' Swishing an imaginary sword, Branwell pursued Emily up the hill. 'Come, Emmii, great genii of Glasstown, tell us!'

'Tell you what?'

'What more you know of the Holmes family,' Branwell persisted. 'What did the fair Martha tell you? Did she confide in you as a sister? What of the mysterious lover? Do you know his name?'

At this Emily stopped in her tracks. 'What did the brother tell *you*?' she countered, suddenly quiet and still.

'Nothing. Not a word. He was close and silent as the grave!' Branwell said with an eerie wail. 'But it is a good tale, is it not, and rich food for our plays, if only we could discover more!'

'I doubt that Mr and Mrs Holmes look at it

in that way,' Emily frowned. 'Besides, Martha seemed flighty and shallow, not worthy of our consideration.'

'But beautiful beyond the ordinary!' Branwell sighed, swooning and acting the lovelorn fool.

'Fair on the outside, but beware vanity and selfishness in such as she,' Emily warned.

'Sour puss – *miaow*! You begin to sound like Charlotte!' Branwell taunted. 'But come, Emmii, what of the young man in the tale? You know more than you say, I'm sure.'

Emily felt her brother follow her as she sidestepped and swept away. It was true that she suspected more, but as yet she had no proof. 'Ask me tomorrow,' was all she would say.

Undeterred, Branwell ran and stepped in her way a second time. 'You are too secretive, Emmii. It is a bad thing in a girl.'

'And you pry too much and feed on shallow gossip!' she retorted. 'It is a bad thing in any human being, boy or girl! But seriously, Branwell, you should see that I am angry now. Leave me alone!'

'Secretive *and* angry!' he mocked. 'Why cannot you be sweet and gentle like Miss Martha!'

Emily turned on him with a savage look. Branwell had prodded deep under her sensitive skin and roused a demon. 'Because I cannot!' she cried. 'I am no curled darling, I have no soft and winning side to my nature, and you of all people know that well enough.'

'Emily, wait!' A strong push had overbalanced Branwell and sent him staggering backwards.

'Whether it is a trick of birth, or the result of this wild moorland life we lead, I cannot tell.' Emily's brown eyes shone fiercely as she finally persuaded her brother to desist. She walked on, flinging one last remark over her shoulder. 'Do not look for womanly ways, for you shall not find them, were you to tear open my heart and study it till doomsday!'

As she walked on, Emily turned over in her mind her suspicions regarding the stranger at the high falls.

Even those without a glimmer of imagination, would find it simple to link the unnamed youth with the groom who had wreaked havoc at Hartcross. For a girl steeped in the tales of Scott, that supposition blossomed into full conviction – Emily was sure that his was the figure, his the face of a spurned lover. His too was the savage, secret presence that haunted the moor, planning his revenge.

And he was also the youth who had chained a poor creature and left it to die – to Emily a crime against nature which could scarcely be believed. She pictured again the dog's dying moments, and cursed the brute who had brought it about.

Now she hurried on with a whole afternoon ahead of her in which to explore the exposed and ruined cottage. She was intent on discovering how recently the youth had been there, and whether or not he had returned after the death of his wretched dog.

Rain clouds had gathered by the time Emily reached the Falls. An east wind swept large, cold drops into her face, and she drew her cloak about her, calling Captain to her side. It would not be long before the rain began in earnest.

Hoping to avoid the worst of the downpour by sheltering in the lee of the horseshoe-shaped falls, Emily retreated out of sight of the shepherd's rude cottage. Behind her, the full waterfall splashed from rock to rock, plunging into a foaming pool overhung by ancient hawthorns and a solitary gnarled oak. The tree, still fiery with autumn leaves, provided refuge from the rain.

'Soon it will stop,' she told Captain with a display of confidence she did not feel. Looking up through the branches at a lowering sky, she feared that the entire afternoon would be wet and dreary. She waited, however, feeling soothed by the constant splash of raindrops against leaves, and by the small black water fowl that swam clear of the weeds and bobbed happily in the turbulent pool.

'We must get a soaking, Captain,' she declared at last. As she had predicted, there was no break in the clouds, nor easing of the rain.

So they set off from the Falls, struggling through bilberry bushes and heather, out onto the bare, rocky surface of the open hillside. Once exposed, she hesitated then pressed on towards the cottage, thinking how she might confront the stranger if he happened to be there, hoping that he would not.

'You are to blame!' she would say. 'What man of Christian sense would leave a dog chained and starving?'

Yet she expected to find the place deserted, thinking it more likely that the stranger had given up his futile pursuit of the rich landowner's daughter, then chained his dog and left for good, unwilling to be encumbered in his flight. 'Better you had hanged the poor creature from the nearest roof beam,' she muttered to herself. 'At least then his end would have been swift!'

And since the ruin would be empty, she would be at liberty to sift through the chipped and rusted belongings by the grate, in search of a clue that would reveal his identity – initials carved on the horn handle of the knife, for instance, or a maker's mark on the old pewter plate.

With such proof she could go back and report to her aunt and sisters that she had indeed found the hiding place of the disgraced groom. Aunt Branwell would be free to tell Mrs Holmes what Emily had discovered – that the untrustworthy servant had not straight away fled the neighbourhood, but had taken up secret residence on the moor top. The trail could then be taken up if the family so wished and the youth would be duly hounded from the district.

I should want him hunted from the face of the earth! she told herself. *Such a man does not deserve to live!*

It was in this mind that she climbed the by-now familiar gate and bade Captain lie still.

Her first thought was to check the site where the dog's body had lain, and so she made her way to the mossy trough and pushed back the nettles. With a sigh of relief she saw that there was no putrefying corpse.

He has been back, she reflected. At least he had the decency to give the creature a decent burial!

At the gate, Captain lay with his head between his paws, whining out his objection at being left behind.

Emily went on, approaching the door to the ruined house, and using all her weight to shift the door, which gave way as before. She scaled the rubble behind the entrance and went quickly on into what had once been the shepherd's kitchen. There, out of the rain, she saw the settle and the ashes in the open grate, and this time, besides the kettle, cup and plate, a rusty spade and a mattock resting against the stone arch of the fireplace.

He makes himself at home, she thought grimly,

imagining the rain sweeping across the moorside and the wind howling through the rafters as the youth had dug a shallow grave for the dead creature.

'What, in the devil's name!' a voice snarled, and he stepped out from behind the settle.

Emily staggered back against the fireplace, pinned there by his savage gaze. The spade clattered and fell to the ground.

'I would raise my hand against such trespassers if I thought it worth my while!' The look showed that he thought her puny and beneath contempt. 'What do you want?' he demanded. 'To give me more thanks, perhaps, or to chastise me?'

She found her voice at last. 'Why would I chastise you, unless you have committed some crime or performed some cruel act?'

'Hah, it speaks! It breaks into my refuge and accuses me!'

'What of the dog?' she insisted, half-afraid, half-angry. She felt her limbs shake and her whole body grow cold.

He stared at her with unblinking eyes. 'So it was you who cut through the creature's rope?' he concluded. 'I found him released from the chain but dead on the ground when I returned. I knew then that some intruder had been here.'

'How was it that you left him to die?' Emily demanded.

'Ah, it is soft hearted! It has feelings for brutes! Then perhaps it would take pity on me!' So saying, the youth strode across the fireplace and took her by the arm. Sitting her on the settle, he bade her listen.

'I went from here on an errand some weeks since,' he told her. 'Never mind the reason – I intended only to be absent for the morning and to be back by noon. However, there were those in the valley who thought otherwise, who discovered and apprehended me, threw me in the lock-up, then brought me before the magistrate in Halifax.

'They held me in prison at Halifax for three days while they argued over the crimes I was supposed to have committed. Long enough for my dog to die of thirst in the heat. Is that enough to satisfy your accursed curiosity and send you on your way?'

Emily felt herself frown. Suddenly the scene changed – if she were to believe him, the dog's death had been an accident and not deliberate cruelty as she'd imagined.

'I see a hundred questions dancing in your brain,' the youth grinned. 'But I mention no names and give you no answers. Only that there was no charge for me to answer other than that of falling deeply and truly in love.'

He paused, lost in reverie. 'They say I stole a heart, but I tell you that it was freely given!'

'The heart of Martha Holmes, was it not?' Emily burst out.

The youth stepped back and narrowed his gaze. 'No names!' he repeated. He stared at her a while, seeming to come to a decision.

She stood up from the settle. 'I tried to save the poor creature,' she murmured regretfully.

'As I said, you have a soft heart, considering this was the brute who had savaged you. And a true heart, it seems, for you kept your promise to me.'

'I did,' she nodded. 'I told no one you were here.'

'And now?'

'Now I do not know. I had supposed you wicked,' she told him openly. 'I had thought to come back and find proof that you were servant to the Holmes family at Hartcross, and then to tell my aunt.'

The youth strode as far as he could across the small room. 'That name again! I warn you, it sets my pulse racing to hear it spoken!'

For a moment Emily thought that he would dash his head against the rough wall to escape hearing more. But he restrained himself and seemed to quieten. 'I will not speak of you,' she promised, hoping to soothe him further.

'Even though I am wicked?'

'It is not as I thought.'

He stretched his lips into a grin without mirth.

'Things seldom are. You would think me a rough servant, would you not?'

'At first,' she agreed, keeping her distance as he skirted the room.

'Yet you would say I speak more nobly than a servant, that perhaps I have received an education beyond that station?'

Emily nodded. All this was true, and it puzzled her.

'A figure that, were it not for the grime on my face and the simplicity of my garb, you would suppose a good match for any young lady of the district? Yes? Well, it is a mystery then, and one that I will not solve with a glib tale for you to carry back home!' So saying, the youth stepped aside from the door where he stood.

'I am free to go?' Emily asked in a shocked, quavering voice.

'Free as air,' he confirmed with a mocking gesture of civility – a bow which a gentleman would give to a lady as he led her onto the dance floor. 'But before you go, I will tell you my name, so that when you hear it mentioned, you may defend it as you see fit.'

'Your name?' Emily echoed. What had this wild and unpredictable stranger to do with a mere name? Somehow she thought him beyond the humdrum and the human.

'My name is Heslington,' he told her. 'You are Emily

Jane Brontë, and so we are on equal footing – name for name. But now, are you friend or foe?'

She looked at him intently. There was danger here, and intrigue. She was treading into forbidden territory. 'Friend,' she answered quietly. 'You may trust me with your life.'

Eight

'What news of the outside world, Ellen?' Charlotte demanded.

She had drawn her friend from Mirfield close to the parlour fire, taken her gloves and bonnet and sat her down, eager for scraps.

'All is well at home at Rydings,' Ellen reported. 'My brother, Henry makes his way in the world. Mama asks after your health, Charlotte, and wishes you to visit us again before Christmas.'

Charlotte blushed with pleasure, though she did not commit herself. Such things depended on Papa. 'We are very quiet here,' she reported in turn.

'Mary Taylor travels to Europe with her papa,' Ellen went on while Anne fussed with the teapot, cups and saucers. 'The girls at school miss you sorely, Charlotte.'

'I doubt that,' came the modest reply.

Impetuously Ellen seized her hand. 'We lack your stories above all!' she declared. 'And without you to look up to and emulate in our lessons, we students fall back sadly in our efforts.'

Emily sat quietly in the corner of the room, watching their talkative guest and soaking up the news. She grimaced when Branwell burst in bearing a brace of pheasants just given to him by the sexton, John Brown. He flung the dead birds onto the mahogany table, not caring that a trickle of blood smeared the polished surface.

'Ellen!' Branwell cried.' How do you do? When are you going to invite Charlotte back to that paradise you call your home, so that I may accompany her on the journey and drink in all those delights once more?'

The girls smiled uneasily, but gentle Ellen laughed. 'Today!' she declared. 'Charlotte knows she is like a sister to me, and my home is hers whenever she cares to make the journey!'

'Then accept, Tallii!' Branwell insisted, swaggering under his heavy cloak. 'And Ellen, take this brace of pheasants home with you as a gift. Better still – let me accompany you on your way. The wind is up and the way to Rydings hard at this time of the year. You will need a fearless companion by your side!'

'Branwell, Ellen has scarcely arrived!' Charlotte protested, jealous of her friend's attention now that her brother had intervened. 'Give us more news, Ellen dear. And Anne, apply to Tabby for cake. Beg her nicely.'

'I'll go,' Emily said, brushing aside her needlework and standing impatiently. But she hesitated in

76

the doorway as the conversation took a different turn.

'We have a new pupil at Roe Head,' Ellen told Charlotte. 'Her name is Martha Holmes. She is a big girl of some fifteen years and a half, and very pretty, Charlotte. She puts us all in the shade, with her fair curls and slender, upright figure!'

'Martha Holmes?' Branwell interrupted eagerly. 'Why, we know her. A real beauty – "Oh, she doth teach the torches to burn bright," in the words of our immortal bard—'

'Does she not go to school in Brussels?' Emily interrupted quickly.

Ellen shook her head. 'There was some such plan, I believe. But her poor father is ill, and her mother did not want to send her so far.' She paused, considering the inquisitive looks on her listeners' faces. 'I see you know more of this story than I supposed!'

'Only that Martha was here. It seems she has caused her papa and mama some distress,' Charlotte sniffed. 'There was a groom, was there not?'

'A scoundrel who stole Martha's heart after the family had taken him in as an orphan and educated him. It is so romantic, is it not?' Daintily sipping her tea, Ellen's eyes darted from one to the other.

'Why a scoundrel?' Emily insisted. All thought of Tabby and cake had fled.

'It is a low creature who betrays a man's generosity and thinks to leap above his station,' Ellen explained. 'Old Mr Holmes had treated the boy almost as a son, though he has a natural one of his own.'

'James,' Anne recalled. 'Well mannered and handsome.'

Ellen nodded. 'Martha speaks of him with disgust, for it was he, James, who discovered the love affair.'

'And so the business is ended,' Charlotte concluded. 'The orphan boy is dismissed. No real harm is done.'

'Except that he did not leave the district immediately,' Ellen told them, and Emily drew near to the fire to listen. 'No, Martha tells us, her eyes aflame with excitement, that he haunted the moor above Hartcross for weeks after his dismissal, all through the autumn. He would arrange secret meetings with her, when she would escape from the confines of Hartcross park under some pretext.'

'Oh!' Anne said, truly shocked.

'He would swear undying love and beg her to leave home and marry him. She said she would rather try to persuade her mama and papa that their feeling was sincere, and so reconcile the family. And so it went on.'

'Until?' Emily quizzed. Her heart beat rapidly as she thought of those stolen moments between the lovers.

'Until the servant was apprehended in Heptonstall and thrown into prison in Halifax, and Martha saw at last the bad nature of the youth. She confesses now that it would humiliate her to marry such a low creature, and she is content finally to follow her parents' wishes.'

'Ah!' Anne said, while Charlotte fixed her glasses on the bridge of her nose and took up her sewing.

'What of the servant?' Emily asked, staring into the flickering flames of the fire.

'Vanished,' Ellen reported. 'Luckily for Martha. A dark, gypsy-like youth by all accounts, with a vicious nature. Martha accepts her mistake and Miss Wooler keeps a strict guard over her new pupil. There is no possibility of elopement now. There, that is the news! And so tell me, Charlotte, how do you pass your days . . . ?'

Though she had kept silent on the occasion of Ellen's visit, Emily's mind dwelt on the situation of the lonely outcast at the falls.

His heart has been wrung out and dashed to the ground! she thought. *How he must suffer!*

'Emily, sweep the rug in the parlour,' Tabby said.

He is alone in the world, with no one to help him.

' "Ainsi, bonsoir, mon enfant!" ' Charlotte wrote, and made Emily and Anne read the words aloud.

Winter sets in. What will he do? Where will he go?

When she awoke each morning, her thoughts flew to

him. While she worked, studied and played, she could not cast him out of her heart.

He was an orphan, without mother or father. Were there brothers and sisters, unknown to him? A family who could take him in now that the Holmes family had rejected him? Perhaps the true parents were still alive and mourning the loss of their child. Say he had been stolen from them as an infant, snatched away from a life of wealth and privilege on a country estate and condemned to suffer poverty on the dark and dismal city streets? Such things were not uncommon.

Or else he had been born in a foreign land, where the sun shone constantly and men made their fortunes in diamond mines, deep in tropical forests, amidst towering, rugged mountains. But Fortune had turned against his family and sent them back across oceans on storm-tossed seas to dreary England. The boy had been lost amongst the vast piles of ship's cargo on the dockside, stolen away by vagabonds as the tide lapped and seagulls soared overhead.

Such was the background that Emily invented for Heslington.

'It is set to snow,' John Brown predicted. The sexton leaned his shotgun against the wash-house wall then engaged in conversation with Tabby. 'The clouds over Oxenhope are heavy with it.'

'Give us November at least without snowfall, for pity's sake!' Tabby sighed. Her hands were red raw with scrubbing the flagstones of the hallway and kitchen. Her back ached and her knees were sore.

Inside the wash-house, the two geese, Diamond and Snowflake, which Emily and Anne had rescued from the moor, protested loudly.

'Is the lad about the place?' John wanted to know. 'I have a mind to take him shooting rabbits down Raikes' Fold.'

'Branwell's nowhere to be seen,' Tabby complained. 'When there's work to do, he makes himself scarce. And you need not grin, John Brown. You're one to lead him astray, as we all know!'

'Shooting rabbits is work,' John protested. 'They run amock in these hollows unless we keep 'em down.'

Just then Emily and Charlotte emerged from the house.

'Aunt says, is there cold beef in the back kitchen?' Charlotte said. 'And shall you make a pie for supper?'

'Do I have two pairs of hands?' Tabby grumbled, drying her hands on her apron and hurrying off. 'Charlotte, you must make the pastry for the pie.'

Emily was left to spread grain on the wash-house floor for the grey geese.

'Nay, they'll never be fattened for Christmas at this

rate,' the sexton observed, his cap pushed well back, a muffler tied high around his chin.

'Then they won't find their way onto your plate, John.' Closing the door behind her, Emily emerged into the yard. She wished he would take himself off and leave her to seize the bundle which she'd hidden in the low rafters of the lean-to stone building.

'It's set to snow,' John said again, idly casting a glance at the heavy clouds. Then he spied Branwell making his way up the narrow alley beside the Black Bull. He hailed him and seized his shotgun, leaving Emily in the yard.

Quickly she reopened the wash-house door and reached up to take down the bundle from the beams. Inside the coarse hessian cloth she'd assembled candles, an old paraffin lamp, a cast-off pair of Papa's leather gloves and a corduroy waistcoat with horn buttons, besides odd lengths of string, a fork and some boot laces. These were intended for Heslington, and her purpose was to pay him a secret visit before the first winter storms.

She set off across the field and over the stile, the bundle tucked under her arm and concealed by her cloak. Already the purple heather had turned to brown in the sharp frosts of November, and the whole hillside bore the marks of relentless wind and rain. Thin streams trickled over black rocks, the pale grass lay flat against the earth. Here and there sheep huddled together in the shelter of a low wall or clump of hawthorns. The sexton had been right about the snow, she found. It fell lightly at first – single flecks of white settling on her cloak and quickly melting – then more thickly on the ground. But it did not worry her. She pressed on up the hill, past Top Withens, until she came to the crag, then turned and walked the ridge to the falls.

The snow covered everything in a layer of pure white. It settled on the bushes, lending new graceful, curves to the land, concealing hollows and clinging to the bark of spindly birch trees. Emily's footprints left a clear trail which was quickly blurred and covered by the fast-falling flakes.

At last she reached the ruined cottage. She saw how the wind drove the snow across the yard and banked up against the crumbling walls. There were no footprints, and no smoke. The gate was barred.

For a while she thought the place deserted and her journey wasted. Heslington had moved on, it seemed. He had heard how the fickle Martha Holmes had deserted him – had given him up and followed her family's wishes. The news had broken him and sent him wandering aimlessly out of the neighbourhood. Emily bit her lip, and her tongue tasted melting snow.

'Since you've made the journey in the snow, you'd best step inside!' The ungracious occupant of the tumble-down cottage emerged suddenly from behind the house.

Emily started, then quickly recovered. She held up the bundle which she had brought.

Heslington came and unbarred the gate. 'Walk in,' he muttered, showing her into the only corner of the cottage that still provided a roof and shelter.

She untied the bundle and spread its contents without speaking.

'I see you are my friend indeed!' Heslington said in a low voice, turning the items this way and that. His smile seemed to convey mild amusement, but he kept his heavily lashed eyes from looking directly at her.

'Your only friend,' Emily revealed. 'Your name is very bad throughout the district.' Then she confessed that she feared he had moved away.

'Not until I have achieved my goal,' he insisted, taking the candles and storing them at one end of the settle. There was no fire in the grate, despite the onset of snow. 'Tell me, do you have news of Martha? Quickly, for I live like an eagle in splendid isolation, and you are my only source of information from the world below.'

'I have heard something,' she began.

'Something to my detriment?' he guessed, drawing her onto the seat and sitting beside her.

She nodded. Close to, she could see the smooth, dark skin of his cheeks, and the way his black hair curled over his forehead. His chin was roughly shaven. 'Martha is now at school near Mirfield,' she said.

Heslington nodded. 'I knew that she was not at Hartcross. My messages have not been taken from our secret hiding-place – a hollow in the trunk of an oak tree at the edge of the park. So the parents have acted to remove their precious daughter from me? How did you learn this?'

While Emily explained about Ellen's visit, Heslington sprang up and paced angrily to and fro. He muttered oaths and caught his breath, thumping his fist against the side of the settle.

'They say she has given you up,' Emily murmured. 'She sees that it would degrade her to marry you now.'

'The devil it would!' he cried. 'This friend of yours – is she honest?'

'Ellen would not be untruthful.'

'And this school – are there bars at each window and a lock on every door?'

'Roe Head is a good school. It is not a prison. My sister, Charlotte has studied there.'

'Roe Head at Mirfield.' He repeated the name, then turned back to Emily. 'You are my good friend, are you not? Then know that Martha would not give me up. They have quietened her with medicines and sent her away, but she will stay true. In her heart she will not renounce me!'

Emily nodded but said nothing. His passion moved her so deeply that she almost cried tears of sympathy.

'She and I are the same!' Heslington insisted. 'Our souls are alike!'

'Then I will do whatever I can to help you both,' Emily promised in a surge of pity.

Heslington seized her hand and eagerly drew her up, tilting her chin towards his face. 'I knew you would say so!'

Her heart beat fast and painful. 'What shall I do?'

He held her small hands between his rough ones, 'I will write a letter. You must take it to her!'

Emily's eyes widened and she gasped.

He clasped her hands more tightly. 'You will be my go-between! Promise!'

Pulling away, she cried out in pain.

'I am sorry, I did not mean to crush your hands. Only say that you will take my letter to Martha!'

'I cannot promise. I do not know how I should achieve it!' Confusion flooded in. Suddenly she wondered, was this really the look of a man in love? His dark eyes glinted, his lips curled back in an eerie smile.

Heslington turned away and strode out of the ruined cottage into the snow. When he came back, he seemed to have regained some composure. There were perfect white snowflakes on his dark head and broad shoulders. 'I have frightened you,' he acknowledged.

'No.' Now that he was calm, Emily denied her fear.

'Martha is my whole world,' he said softly. 'I cannot live without her.'

His gentle avowal finally made up Emily's mind for her. 'Write your letter,' she said. 'Martha shall know of your true feelings. If I have strength and wit to do it, I shall deliver your message to her!'

Nine

' "Now when Jesus was born in Bethlehem of Judaea in the days of Herod the king, behold there came wise men from the east to Jerusalem." ' Anne overcame her stammer to give a fluent rendering of the lesson before her sisters, brother and aunt. She had rehearsed it over and over, until she was word-perfect.

'Prettily done, Anne!' Aunt Branwell declared. 'Your papa shall know how hard you have worked.'

It was three weeks before Christmas. Mr Brontë was much taken up with visiting the sick and looking after his flock. Despite the wintry weather, a bout of typhoid fever had laid low some far-flung parishioners. Two had died, and he was presently away from home, ministering to the bereaved.

'Shall I read in church?' Anne wondered. 'Is my voice strong enough?'

'Strong, and clear as an angel's!' Charlotte declared. The season brought her contentment, with the choirboys' rehearsal of carols in the vestry, and many a consultation with Tabby in the kitchen over the roasting of game birds, the basting of hams and the boiling of puddings.

As Anne rehearsed, Emily roamed restlessly from room to room. She had given her promise, yet Heslington's unsealed letter still lay undelivered amongst her pile of papers containing her poems and the latest episodes of the Gondal tales.

'Do not fail me!' he had begged in agony.

She had hurried away through the snow, stumbling into hollows and arriving home chilled to the bone to her aunt's chiding and Tabby's loud consternation.

'Eh, child, have you no sense? Only fools or those up to no good go out on the moors on days like these.'

'Emily's no fool!' Branwell had cut in. 'She has brains enough for the whole lot of us.'

'Then she was up to no good,' Charlotte had pronounced severely as Emily had unlaced her snow-clogged boots by the kitchen fire.

But Emily had kept the letter close and revealed it to no one.

Now four whole weeks had gone by without an opportunity to deliver it to Martha Holmes, and Emily's agitation over it rose daily.

'I will take Captain up onto the moor,' she announced when Aunt Branwell took herself and her sewing up to her room, and Branwell, Anne and Charlotte sat themselves at the parlour table and took up pen and ink.

Anne looked disappointed. 'And shall the Gondals continue with their discovery of the the Interior?' she asked, her quill pen made from a rook's feather hovering over the tiny sheet of paper.

Emily nodded.

' "*Why, when I hear the stormy breath*
Of the wild winter wind . . ." ' Anne read out the beginning of a new poem from the page.

' " . . . Rushing o'er the mountain heath . . ." ' Emily suggested, reaching for Captain's lead and calling him from the hearth.

The girl and the dog walked, as they always did, across the rough fields at the back of the parsonage, over the stiles and onto the moor.

On this day, however, Emily chose not to walk beyond the narrow falls where she and Charlotte often rested – a spot less exposed and closer to home than the more rugged Haygarth Falls. As Captain foraged through the dark heather, she found she could not rid her thoughts of Heslington's letter, and it was probably this that made her believe that she was not alone. It was a sensation of being watched, of eyes following her every movement as she came to a halt on the thick stone slab across the stream. And yet there was nothing but open sky above and the wide expanse of moors and fields below.

'Is anybody there?' she said out loud, drawing her cloak about her.

Captain checked his wandering and trotted to her, looking to right and left.

The clear water tumbled over the worn rocks, rooks sailed high in the grey sky.

'No,' she decided, striding on. But still the sense of being observed continued. *It is inside my head!* She told herself. *Eyes watching. A reproach being made.* She stopped again beside Top Withens farmhouse with its wide yard and a black-and-white dog chained at the gate. The chimney smoked, the doors and mullioned windows were shut tight.

How am I to deliver this letter? she asked herself. *The parsonage and the moors are my world, together with the church and our tiny town. I never stray from Haworth into the wider world.*

Perhaps she should trust a messenger with the precious letter? This recurring idea fluttered feebly through her mind then settled into dusty inaction. Who? Whom should I trust? There was Sally Mosley, who went with her mother into Keighley on market day. There was John Brown, who took the open cart to Halifax. But they were both prone to idle chatter.

Walking on as dusk drew in, Emily passed a blackened pillar known as Sutcliffe's Folly, built by soldiers who had returned from the wars against Napoleon and found themselves without useful employment. The landowner, William Sutcliffe, had set them building in order to occupy idle hands.

Still without a solution to her problem, Emily bent her path homewards.

When she arrived, she found her brother and sisters still wrapped up in their unreal worlds.

'Viscount Elrington has betrayed his brothers and schemed against the Glasstown Confederacy,' Charlotte reported with an excited smile. 'His ambitions have grown unmanageable. Bany has decided there is to be another civil war!'

For once, Emily did not respond. Instead, she sat at her place and unfolded her papers with a distracted air.

Anne rose and went for a fresh candle, while Branwell's pen scratched out a portrait of the treacherous viscount.

'What is this?' Branwell asked Emily, reaching over to take up Heslington's folded letter. Emily had been less careful than usual to conceal it at the bottom of the pile. ' "My beloved Martha," ' he read, ' "I am in hell without you! I find I have to tell my heart to beat and my lungs to draw breath, for loneliness overcomes me and makes me wish for oblivion . . ." '

Emily gasped and tried to snatch back the paper. She had not opened it, nor read any part of it, believing its contents to be the almost sacred expression of a deeply felt love to which no outsider should gain access. 'Give it back!' she demanded, her face white with anger.

Branwell held the letter at arm's length. 'It is a love letter! Why, Emily!' he mocked carelessly. 'Who has fallen in love with whom in Gondal? I thought that the inhabitants were too busy exploring the interior to bother with affairs of the heart!' He returned the letter to his sister before going back to examine the portrait, which he planned to take to the Black Bull to show to his crony, John Brown.

Charlotte waited until he was gone. ' "My beloved Martha"?' she repeated sharply. 'This is written to Martha Holmes, is it not?'

Emily glared at her.

'How did you come by this? What game is being played?' Charlotte demanded, seizing the letter, her hand trembling with pent-up emotion.

'Come, Charlotte, give me the paper. It is not your business, nor mine neither.' Emily stood tall and tried to pass off the incident.

'It is my duty to keep you from harm,' Charlotte protested. 'I fear you have been rash, Emily, though I cannot make out exactly how.'

The puzzled expression on Charlotte's short-sighted face brought a grim smile to Emily's own. 'Give me the letter,' she insisted, so fiercely that Charlotte handed it back.

Quickly taking a stick of red wax and melting it at the guttering candle flame, she sealed the letter with the Brontës' own stamp. 'There!' she exclaimed, satisfied that its contents were beyond them both.

'What have you done?' Charlotte gripped the edge of the table. 'Worse; what do you intend to do?'

'Hush!' Emily warned as Anne returned minus the new candle.

'Tabby says we must do without,' Anne reported, shuffling her own papers into a neat pile and tying them with green ribbon. 'I have promised to read to Aunt,' she sighed, disappearing again from the room.

The low candle spluttered and cast flickering shadows on the grey walls.

'Charlotte, you must say nothing of this!' Emily pleaded. She saw that she must confess everything and win her elder sister onto her side. 'Two hearts depend upon it. If you reveal what you have seen, there will be no remedy!'

'You talk in riddles!' Charlotte complained, sitting weakly at the table. 'Tell me how you come to be go-between for Martha Holmes and her disgraced lover!'

So Emily reluctantly recounted the first chance meeting with Heslington at Haygarth Falls – how his vicious cur had fought with Captain, how she had come between them, been wounded and fallen into a faint. How she had been revived by a dark stranger.

'Dark stranger?' Charlotte echoed. 'This is the groom dismissed by Mr Holmes, Emily. He is a scoundrel with whom no respectable person would associate!'

'He is in love with Martha Holmes!' Emily insisted, telling Charlotte all that she had learned. 'And Martha loves him in return!'

'Not according to Ellen,' Charlotte reminded her. 'It seems that when Miss Martha saw that she was to be disinherited, she quickly fell out of love and in line with her father's wishes.'

'What does Ellen know of affairs of the heart?' Emily retorted. 'Come Charlotte, be honest – Ellen is but an innocent girl from a sheltered family, with no knowledge of the world.'

Charlotte laughed bitterly. 'And what are we, Emily?'

'Not so innocent, at least.'

Charlotte was silent a while, then shook her head. 'I must tell Papa,' she resolved.

This drove Emily into intense, cold fury. 'You are a faint-hearted soul,' she accused. 'You call it duty, Charlotte, and cloak it in mealy-mouthed religion, but it is cowardice that drives you to this course of action. It is because you dare not let the heart speak!'

The words stunned Charlotte. 'You say this to me?' she muttered in disbelief.

'Yes. Duty is your guiding principle. I must obey! It flattens your spirit, Charlotte, and makes your life grey and ordinary!'

'Because it is the way of our Lord.' The words, even as she spoke them, sounded hollow even to Charlotte.

Emily turned away scornfully. 'You wear blinkers like the horse that pulls the closed cart!'

This time Charlotte rounded on her. She flew to Emily's side of the table and pulled at her arm. 'It is cruel to say so! I have a heart as large as yours, Emily, though I don't let it be seen.'

Emily looked down at the small hand gripping her own. 'Then act upon it, Charlotte,' she said more gently. 'Help me fulfil this promise, and no harm shall come, you'll see.'

So, against her better judgment, Charlotte sent a message to Ellen Nussey at Roe Head.

'My dearest Ellen, Emily and I wish to visit you, not at home, but at school before Christmas. We have gifts and letters for you and the Miss Woolers. Let me know how we should manage this. Shall we arrive by cart and take tea with you and the other girls? It would be delightful to see you and them, and to exchange seasonal news. Send a reply by this boy from the village. From your real friend, Charlotte Brontë.'

'To Roe Head?' Aunt Branwell quizzed, her thin eyebrows disappearing under her heavy front of false curls. 'It is scarcely the weather for travelling.'

'To see Ellen Nussey?' Papa repeated. 'My dear Charlotte, you are not strong. I fear you would not stand the journey.'

'I shall take care of her,' Emily promised. It was as if she held her breath day in, day out, until the mission to deliver the letter was accomplished. It was only after much persuasion that Charlotte had agreed to be her accomplice, and had devised this secret means of passing Heslington's passionate declaration of love into Martha Holmes's hand.

'Nay, they've taken leave of their senses at last,' Tabby declared, shaking her head and retiring to her kitchen.

In the end and in the face of puzzled disapproval, it could only be achieved by Branwell's volunteering to guide and guard the two girls.

'Papa, you must let Charlotte wrap up well and not think that she will expire in the least puff of wind!' he declared. 'But Emily need not come now that I am to go.'

'Emily must accompany me,' Charlotte insisted. 'I have promised to show her Roe Head.'

Mr Brontë approved this point. 'Go, Emily!' he declared, one eye to the future as ever. 'And be sure to show Miss Wooler that you have an intellect at least equal to Charlotte's, for going as a teacher to Roe Head is not the worst fate that could await you!'

Emily endured the prospect in silence, as she did Branwell's presence on the journey.

They set off at six o'clock on the Wednesday morning, exactly two weeks before Christmas Day, with the ground frozen hard as iron and a hoar frost glittering on the branches of the trees.

' "In the dead of night Elrington spirited away his beloved mistress and her maid!" ' Branwell proclaimed. ' "Theirs was to be a life of adventure. The mountains enveloped them and concealed their flight. Great glaciers towered to either side, the sound of a distant avalanche drowned out the constant sobbing of the frightened servant!" '

Emily sat in silence, nursing Heslington's letter inside the leather bag containing Charlotte's Christmas gifts. As the sky lightened and the road grew unfamiliar, she rehearsed the moment in the schoolroom when she would draw Martha Holmes to one side and quietly release the paper into its owner's keeping.

Beside her, Charlotte kept still and quiet as the grave, while Branwell, sitting up front with Henry Poole, the cartman, kept up his tale of elopement. ' "My dearest Rogue!" Zenobia whispered. "I have cast myself into your arms and forsaken society for your sake!"

Elrington embraced his beloved in his manly arms. "And I shall never desert you!" he declared.'

They passed through villages just waking to the winter's day, by the large new mills built by fast-running water, their giant wheels turning. And still Emily's mind ran on the first passage of Heslington's passionate letter. '*My beloved Martha, I am in hell without you!*' Near Dewsbury town, Branwell left off his tale and turned to the girls. 'Tell me,' he said with a confident smile, 'do you not think me the handsomest man in all Yorkshire?'

'Very handsome,' Charlotte said evenly. 'And very boastful.'

'No but, would you not be flattered if a man such as I came courting?'

Emily frowned at his bright red hair and long side whiskers, his thin, pinched face and pale complexion. 'Whom do you see as the object of your attentions today?'

Branwell grinned. 'I have not yet decided. It may be Ellen, for she has been in my sights for many months, and she is a quiet, good girl. Or it may be Miss Martha Holmes, she of the wondrous golden curls, whose papa's wealth could keep me in comfort for the rest of my life. There again, I'll wager there are any number of rich young ladies at Miss Wooler's school!'

'Giddup!' Poole flicked his whip against the horse's grey flank and turned her down a narrow lane. The day had grown bright and clear, revealing robins perched in the hedges, and long, straight furrows ploughed into the bare fields beyond.

'Branwell, you must not say or do anything to make us ashamed!' Charlotte insisted, her pulse racing as Roe Head school came into view on a rising slope. It was a three storeyed, roomy house with four chimney stacks, approached by a curved drive and backed by tall trees.

They were greeted at the door by Ellen, and by the short, stout, graceful figure of Miss Margaret Wooler herself.

Miss Wooler greeted Charlotte warmly and led the way into an airy entrance hall where the sisters and Branwell took off their cloaks.

'The girls are still at breakfast,' the head teacher explained, taking the visitors into the empty schoolroom.

Emily gazed at the long table strewn with books and at the bay window through which she could see a file of girls marching across a courtyard towards the main building. While Miss Wooler asked her old pupil about her studies and the prospect of her one day returning to Roe Head as a teacher, Emily stared at the etched pictures on the walls of famous buildings in Rome and Paris, and at the large globe set against a wall lined with leather-bound books.

'And Branwell,' Miss Wooler went on, smiling at a suddenly ill at ease, tongue-tied boy. 'I hear you are to be an artist?'

Branwell grunted out his answer as the schoolgirls entered the room. There was an excited chorus when they spotted Charlotte in her old grey dress and glasses, her hair frizzed as usual into an unbecoming frame for her thin face. Before long they had descended on her and were demanding news of life outside the school.

'Fifteen minutes!' Miss Wooler warned. 'And then you must get to your lessons.' She smiled kindly at Emily as she left the room to take Branwell on a tour of the grounds.

Surrounded by girls, all chattering and laughing, Emily found that her heart almost failed her. She wished to run away and hide, to make herself invisible – anything rather than be dragged into the crowd. And yet she had a task to execute – one that could transform the life of the outcast on the moor.

So she steeled herself and sought out the figure of Martha Holmes. The newest pupil was standing slightly to one side, wearing a black ribbon garter-style around her shoulder. Her hands were clasped in front of her, her face blank and giving no sign of recognition of Emily or Charlotte.

As Charlotte demanded the leather bag containing

her gifts, Emily slid Heslington's letter from the front pocket and concealed it in the folds of her skirt. Then she approached Martha and nervously reminded her of their meeting in Haworth.

Martha raised her fair eyebrows the merest fraction. 'The clergyman's daughter,' she recollected with faint distaste.

Emily felt her face grow hot. 'You were to go to school in Brussels, I believe?'

Another small reaction – this time, a nod of the fair head, 'But my father wants me near him. Or rather, he needs to keep a close eye on me, lest I run away!'

Emily's lids flickered down then she met the proud girl's gaze. But before she could speak, Martha let out a flood of complaint.

'This school is a prison! The teachers are no better than jailers and fools! Look how they award me the black ribbon for unladylike manners – why, they would not recognise a lady, not they! What do they know of anything but dry grammar and geography? And the pupils here are mere farmers' daughters and destined to be old maids!'

'It seems you would have preferred Brussels,' Emily said with a wry smile. She wondered again, but more forcefully this time, how a passionate man like Heslington could throw away his heart on such a bad tempered, shallow creature. Yet, she must fulfil her promise and deliver the letter. So she drew Martha into a quiet corner of the room.

'Why so secretive?' The bigger girl had resisted and pulled away. 'You are an odd child. Come, say what you mean and have done!'

Carefully Emily drew Heslington's letter from her skirt. 'It is from *him*!' she whispered.

Martha frowned and stared at the paper. 'What is this seal?' she demanded, seizing the letter and turning it this way and that, so openly that some of the other girls turned inquisitively from Charlotte.

'It is from Heslington!' Emily warned. *My beloved Martha, I am in hell without you!*

The name shocked Martha into silence at last, and she hid the paper behind her back.

'You have seen him?' she demanded, her grey eyes round and staring.

Emily nodded. 'He has taken refuge in an abandoned cottage on the moor. He is tormented by your absence.'

At this a smile played on Martha's lips. 'He is in torment,' she repeated.

'You must read the letter and send a reply,' she urged. 'I cannot go back without one!'

'This is a fine Christmas gift you bring!' Martha declared. 'Well, it has taken him long enough to find me, and so he must wait for my reply!'

Emily frowned. 'You don't understand. He lives like

a fugitive on the moor top, without proper shelter. It is the dead of winter. You must send him word!'

' "Must"!' Martha echoed. She reflected a while, as if planning her move. 'I will read the letter before you and your brother and sister depart,' she decided. 'When do you leave?'

'At noon.'

'Then I will peruse it during history, as I say, and will send a spoken reply, which you may deliver.'

'I?' Emily faltered.

'Yes, since you relish the role of messenger between us. I will tell you what to say, and you must be sure to repeat it to him word for word.'

With this, Martha Holmes left Emily and rejoined the throng of girls.

Ten

'I fear we are in too deep!' Charlotte whispered to Emily on their way home from Roe Head. 'Ellen suspected that all was not well, that the reason for our visit was not the simple exchange of gifts.'

Emily sat back under the coarse canvas cover of the cart which rattled and rumbled along the rough road into Haworth. She was glad when Branwell leaped down and raced ahead on foot. 'You did not tell Ellen our secret?' she murmured back.

'Not a word.'

'Good.' Like Charlotte, Emily had been shaken by the day's events and her opinion of Martha Holmes had not improved. Indeed, she now suspected her of toying with Heslington's affections and creating misery for him by returning promises which she would never keep.

'Tallii, my heart aches,' she confessed as they ascended the steep, cobbled hill. 'I do not find anything in Martha Holmes to like or admire. I wish it were otherwise – that she possessed a true spirit and a loyal heart – but I see only vanity and selfishness.'

Charlotte considered the opinion silently. 'She is not liked at Roe Head,' she said at last. 'Mary Taylor mistrusts her. Even sweet Ellen finds few kind words to say, except that Martha is away from home for the first time and does not know how to make friends.'

'She bade me carry a message,' Emily confessed, looking out at the weavers' cottages to either side of the main street.

Martha Holmes had read Heslington's impassioned love letter as promised, and calmly composed her reply. She had sought Emily out on the driveway, as Ellen and Mary had said their fond goodbyes to Charlotte.

'You will remember what I say to you,' she'd instructed. 'You will tell Heslington that I am pining away for the loss of him. Do not interrupt. I scarcely sleep and I have left off eating. If we do not meet again, I shall die.'

'Is this the truth?' Emily had asked.

'Truth or no, you will say this to him – that I long to be rescued and fall into his arms once more. That this time I will not hesitate, but I will defy Papa and marry him.'

Emily had drawn a sharp breath.

'Keep your wits about you,' Martha had warned, seeing that the rough cart had arrived to take the visitors away. 'My future depends upon you remembering these words. Repeat them to me now.'

'You are pining for the loss of him,' Emily recounted. 'You neither sleep nor eat. You will die if you two do not meet again.'

'Good!' Martha nodded. 'Go on.'

'You long to be rescued,' Emily stammered. She came to a halt over the next part.

'And to fall into his arms,' Martha insisted. 'Be sure to tell him that. And then?'

'You will defy your papa and marry him!' Emily gasped.

'Good again! There, that is enough. Only say that I will send another message soon. Do not look so scared!' the older girl had scoffed. 'Should you fail, there are other messengers besides you!'

But Emily had climbed into the cart, promising that she would fulfil her part. At the last minute, Branwell had appeared nonchalantly from behind the house and ordered the cartman to hurry away. There had been the waving and Ellen's tears, the final exchange of Christmas greetings and Miss Wooler's kind farewell.

But now both Emily and Charlotte were shaken by their experiences. 'I say we are in too deep,' Charlotte insisted, fearing Anne's eager questions about their day and Aunt Branwell's sharp glance. 'How are we to face the others with a clear conscience, knowing what we know?'

'Ah, conscience!' Emily said with mock seriousness, but her attempt at humour was hollow – she was in no mood to chide Charlotte. After all, she carried her own burden of duty towards the outcast. 'Say nothing, Tallii,' she sighed, waiting until the cart lurched to a halt before she stepped onto the icy pavement. 'I will fulfil my part of the bargain by taking this message to Heslington.'

'And must you?' With a dry rustle of skirts Charlotte descended from the cart.

'I must, and soon!'

'And then?'

'Then I shall have played my part.'

Emily escaped from the house as soon as she was able. Martha Holmes's words weighed on her conscience. Until they were delivered, she could scarcely move or breathe.

So she set out the next morning, a purposeful figure leaving behind the town and ascending the hill until she reached the lower fall, where she rested and tried to compose herself.

If only Martha were a worthy lover for Heslington! But no; she was not worth a moment's loss of sleep over, let alone the ruin of a man's good name and occupation!

So thinking, and still agitated by the task ahead, Emily picked up her skirt and walked on.

She had not reached Timble Crag before the man she was seeking appeared before her.

Heslington came striding down the hillside with the wind behind him, jumping down ledges and brushing aside thorn bushes in his path. He did not speak, but instead seized Emily's hand and drew her into the shelter of a rock. His look bored into her soul. 'You have kept me waiting for what seems like an eternity!' he complained. 'It is beyond bearing!'

'I bring a message,' Emily gasped, anxious to get this over and be gone.

He put out his hand to receive it.

'It is not written down. It is that she pines away without you. She neither sleeps nor eats.' Quickly she launched into the carefully rehearsed speech.

'Hah!' Heslington's inarticulate cry pierced the silence. 'What else?'

Emily's intense shyness prevented her from conveying the phrase about Martha's longing to fall into his arms, but she imparted the rest. 'She will die unless you rescue her.'

'And she will marry me?'

Emily nodded. 'You must expect another message soon.'

And now it was done and she must hurry away, but he detained her, pressing for more information, refusing to believe that Martha could leave him without a firm plan. 'You say at any rate that she will defy her father for me. They said she would not, but they are fools that believe that love does not cross the puny boundaries of society.'

'I did not doubt it,' Emily said, trying to soothe his desperate state. He breathed heavily, almost choking on his words. 'You must be patient now. Martha will send news.'

'How? Who will bring another message? Who knows where to find me?'

Emily shook her head. 'You must trust her.'

Heslington narrowed his gaze. 'She makes me wait, damn her! Go again and tell her I will not dance attendance forever!'

The sudden change of mood made Emily dizzy – that, and the blustering wind. 'I cannot go back to Roe Head!' she declared.

'Cannot. Will not. You are a poor friend after all!'

'A better one than you might find elsewhere,' she said more calmly. 'There are those who would not brave this wild wind.' And whirling, stormy feelings, she might have added.

Her remark brought him to his senses. 'Go then,' he said abruptly, standing clear of the boulder. 'You have done me a service, for which I thank you.'

'I have not brought bad news either. I am sure that Martha is sincere.'

'And how would she not be?' Heslington asked, standing in the full force of the wind, looking out across the hillside. 'We will defy the old man together, she and I. We will have our pound of flesh.'

Emily emerged from the shelter. 'I wish you happiness,' she murmured, but her words were whipped from her mouth and found no answering smile.

'I like a girl with spirit!' Branwell crowed. He was holed up in the Black Bull with John Brown and his drinking cronies, boasting about his recent trip to Roe Head.

'Aye, and a father with plenty of land to boot,' Aaron Cheevers growled, tapping his pipe out at the grate. Old and rheumaticky as he was, the weaver kept in touch with village gossip about the Holmes family.

'How did you worm your way into her good books?' the sexton wanted to know.

His amused interest pushed Branwell into yet more indiscretion. 'Easy!' he cried. 'I strode about the frosty garden, minding my own business, but looking bold and jaunty. After Miss Martha had finished her serious talk with my sister Emily, she sought me out.'

'Oh-ho!' Aaron chuckled, his throat thick with phlegm.

'And why should she not?' Branwell declared. 'How many times has Martha Holmes been put in the way of a talented, educated individual like me? Why, she lives like a recluse at Hartcross – her father has seen to that!'

'So she sought you out?' John prompted. He'd known Branwell ever since he was a babe in arms, and it tickled him to see how the ridiculous boy bragged and swaggered. 'Then what?'

'Knowing that Emily was not bold, she formed a plan with me, to execute her escape!'

'Never!' Aaron growled.

'She did! She took me to one side, down an avenue of beech trees, saying that she could not rely on Emily, so she must trust me with a deep secret which I must never tell, on pain of my life!'

'Which is why you now broadcast it far and wide,' Aaron muttered under his breath. 'Nay, I'd not trust you with a brass farthing, Branwell, never mind my life!'

'Go on!' John bade him. 'Tell us, Branwell, how are you and she to – er-hum – execute Martha Holmes's escape?'

'Where is Branwell?' Mr Brontë asked, tapping the casement clock on the landing of the stairs.

It was five days after the visit to the school. The cold weather had eased its grip and the approach to Christmas slid by in a grey, damp mist which hung over the houses of the town and wound its way through the narrow streets.

'It is well past the time when he should be studying his latin.'

'Let me go and bring him home, Emily volunteered, giving over her duster to Anne, and hurrying from the house. She cast an uneasy glance at Charlotte as she went.

For days now Branwell had been acting strangely, with one eye always on the window overlooking the side lane, or else hovering amongst the gravestones in the graveyard, looking down towards the main street. Emily dated the behaviour back to their visit to Roe Head, and felt increasingly certain that Branwell was up to no good.

After a good deal of anxious searching up and down the alleyways between the weavers' cottages, she came out onto the main street beside the inn. There was a bustle of horses and carts, the echo of clogs and hooves on the cobbles, the smell of smoke and the feel of cold, wet mist in the air. Amidst the busy scene she caught sight of her brother deep in conversation with Henry Poole, the cartman.

'I did the job. I waited as I was told, when I was told, in the place you told me, and now I want payment for my pains!' the man, Poole, was protesting as Emily hurried up.

Branwell had his back to her and spoke passionately. 'You are a damned fool, Henry. It was a simple errand, was it not? And yet you come back all the way from Mirfield without your passenger!'

'The lady did not meet me as planned. What was I to do?'

'Wait a little longer. Make enquiries. Now all is lost!' Branwell turned away in exasperation and came face to face with Emily. When he saw her, his expression changed from anger to guardedness.

She didn't have time to interrogate him, however, because the clatter of hooves up the street announced a hasty visitor. Emily glanced down the hill to see a cloaked rider, his hat pulled well down, reining back his horse and jumping to the ground.

'Brontë!' the newcomer cried, seeking Branwell out by his red hair and accosting him before he had time to flee.

Branwell resisted with a wild thrust of his forearm which knocked off the taller youth's hat to reveal none other than James Holmes.

'I should whip you to within an inch of your life!' Holmes declared, recovering and pinning Branwell back against the stone door jamb to the inn.

Branwell's face twisted in pain. 'Leave off! Henry, come to my aid, damn you!'

The cartman stood by, arms folded, stolidly watching the drama.

'What do you intend – to bring my family to ruin?'

Holmes raged. 'You would assist my sister in her lunatic plan, would you?'

At this Emily sprang forward. 'Branwell, tell me what you have done!'

Still pressing him into the corner, James Holmes cast a sideways glance at her. 'He has only sent a covered cart to fetch my sister away from her school, on the pretext of visiting our poor father! In truth, she planned to run away and meet up with her lover here in Haworth!' he cried.

'Tell me you did not!' Emily insisted. 'Branwell, you have done no such thing!'

'He has. He has plotted with Martha to bring her here to be reunited with that scoundrel, Heslington!'

By now, a large group of onlookers, including old Aaron Cheevers and Sally Mosley, had gathered. There was a gasp at mention of the disgraced groom's name.

'Aye, Heslington!' Holmes repeated. 'The rogue who would steal away half my own fortune with his lies and deceit.'

'No!' Emily could not refrain from springing to her friend's defence. 'You misjudge him! I believe it is a case of true love!'

And now, as Martha's brother faltered, Branwell was able to slip from his grasp. 'There is the real culprit!' he declared, pointing to Emily. 'My own part is small compared with hers, for she carried the first letter from

Heslington. Your sister merely asked me to send a cart on this day, at a certain time, to a certain place.'

'Aye, sir, so that she could defy her family, and most especially her father, who even now lies dangerously ill!'

As Holmes turned from one to the other, Sally Mosley took it upon herself to run unnoticed up the hill to tell Mr Brontë that Branwell was brawling in the street.

'Well, the plan has misfired,' James said, mastering his anger at last. 'My sister was apprehended by Miss Wooler as she sneaked through a side door. She was made to confess, and was taken straight away to Hartcross, where she will remain from now on.' Emily flinched at the news. It seemed that all was lost. She pictured Heslington's despair.

'Aye, she is safe from harm's way, no thanks to you!' James Holmes told her with grim finality. 'And I am here to inform your father of the part you have both played in your ignorance. For you have piled up trouble on an ailing, elderly man, and brought his only daughter to the edge of ruin.'

Eleven

'Children, this is a sorry state.' In the parlour after James Holmes's visit, Aunt Branwell presided over a subdued group.

Anne's head was bent over the hemming of a petticoat, Charlotte had a book of Byron's poems open but unread on her lap. Emily meanwhile stood by the tall window overlooking the churchyard, while Branwell sulked in a corner.

'Your poor papa!' their aunt sighed. 'Think of his name in the district, and how we shall all be regarded as a laughing stock.' Breaking through her normal reserve, Aunt Branwell spoke her feelings. 'They will gossip from here to Halifax about the widowed parson and his unruly offspring, how he delivers Sunday sermons on our Lord's justice but cannot exercise authority over his own brood. Why, his son is no better than a fool, and his daughters are lost in a fairy-tale world of their own making. 'Tis a shame, girls!'

Tears fell onto Anne's white lawn, Charlotte closed her eyes and felt her head swim.

'The fault lies with me.' Emily declared. 'The others do not deserve blame.'

'Very noble, Emily.' Branwell kicked at his chair leg, sitting sprawled against the wall. 'And much good may your high mindedness do you.'

She turned on him. 'And just how did you think to enact this hot-headed plan of yours?' she demanded. 'Once you had brought Martha here to Haworth, how was she to find Heslington without my help, pray?'

Branwell shrugged and Charlotte intervened. 'That is nothing now, Emily. It is past. I felt from the start that this would end badly. I should have listened to my own conscience.'

'Indeed you should,' Aunt nodded. She stood before the fire, sighing and wringing her hands until the door handle turned and Mr Brontë walked in.

All heads turned. Branwell sat upright and Charlotte closed her book.

Their father looked slowly from one to the next, his gaze resting finally on Emily. 'You have deceived me,' he said quietly.

Charlotte felt her nerves stretch and snap. 'Papa!'

He raised his hand in warning. 'Emily has deceived me and brought shame upon your mother's memory. My poor Maria!'

Anne began to sob, Emily to pace up and down.

'James Holmes has told me everything,' Mr

Brontë went on in a voice without emotion. His tired, lined face seemed almost strangled by his high, white cravat. 'His sister has confessed her plan to elope and has described the part played by you girls, and by you, Branwell. I have asked him to accept my apologies and reminded him of your untutored youth and inexperience in the world.'

Emily's skirt swished against the table as she turned.

'I offered this in poor excuse for your behaviour, mark you, and prayed that he would convey my remarks to his father and mother.'

'Did James accept the apology?' Aunt Branwell asked. ' 'Tis a wonder if he did, for it is my humble opinion that the Holmes family has every right to continue angry and to exact some recompense.'

Mr Brontë listened then nodded. 'James seemed calmer at least, and is gone back to Hartcross. For now we have done all we can do.'

'Then Anne, go to Tabby and say that we are ready for supper,' Aunt Branwell ordered. 'Charlotte, lay the table. Emily, feed the dogs. Branwell, comb your hair and make yourself decent. Tonight you will go to bed without candles. Tomorrow, we will consider how we may make amends.'

That night Charlotte brushed out her hair with hands

almost too weak to move. Shame paralysed her and made the world seem dark.

Emily sat in her nightdress with her back to the bedroom window and watched her. Anne was already in bed, lying still and unhappy, hoping in vain that the present shroud of misery would soon lift.

'Say something,' Emily urged. 'Tallii, I can't bear it if you refuse to speak!'

But there was only the sound of the brush running through Charlotte's brown hair and the faint rush of wind through the trees overlooking the churchyard.

'Are you angry?' Emily pleaded. 'Yes, I see you are. But Charlotte, you did not speak with Heslington yourself. His name is condemned far and wide, but one word with him would convince you that he deserves our help!'

Charlotte laid down her brush. 'Do not excuse what we have done,' she said in a voice so soft that it could hardly be made out.

Emily sat in the narrow window recess and drew her knees to her chest. 'Tell me, Anne, what should you have done if you had been him? Should you have accepted banishment and the loss of the one you loved?'

'Emmii, I don't know!'

'Or should you have fought to win her back?'

'Don't answer, Anne,' Charlotte cut in. 'We know, Emily, that you favour the outcast – it is in your nature to rescue wild things from the moor and nurse them back to health. But this is a man, not a wounded pigeon or hawk. He is not injured. He is someone who has acted wrongly and must be punished for it.'

'According to whose laws?' Emily demanded. 'You do not know him, else you would not say so!'

'And you do?' Charlotte scoffed. 'You know this creature who stands condemned, who would defy everyone and everything to follow his own desires!'

'Yes, I know how it seems.' Emily was too restless to stay seated by the small window. She got up and stood behind Charlotte at the dressing table. 'At first I too thought him bad, for he is fierce and angry, and he looks so wild. But you would not say these things if you had seen him as I have, in his rough shelter, tortured by his situation, yet still following his heart!'

Charlotte sighed and stood up to face her. 'You are sure, in spite of everything that has happened today, that Heslington is true?'

True enough to endure a winter at Haygarth Falls. Constant when he was thrown into prison and dragged before the magistrate. Desperate for news of Martha. Passionate in his declaration of love. 'I am sure,' Emily replied.

'Then God help us,' Charlotte murmured, looking out at the crescent moon.

He was out there still, enduring the cold, waiting for news.

'And God help *him*,' Emily added quietly.

Hartcross Manor lay in a valley overlooked by wooded hills. Its situation would have given it a green, sheltered appearance during summer months, but in late December all looked harsh and grey, from the tall, castellated walls surrounding its large park to the porticoed frontage and narrow, mullioned windows of the house itself.

Charlotte and Emily had survived the rough journey from Haworth in a state of extreme agitation, though Branwell had put on a careless air and insisted on passing comment on any sight worthy of note on the way.

'There is the low road to Oxenhope, and there the lane to Norton, where John Brown's sister, Hannah, keeps the inn. That signpost points to Heptonstall.'

'I should think you better employed in rehearsing what you must say to Mr and Mrs Holmes,' Mr Brontë would say. Or else he would sit in bitter silence next to Henry Poole, peering short sightedly over his spectacles.

'Girls, you are not to speak unless spoken to,' he instructed Emily and Charlotte. 'You are to let your brother apologise on your behalf, and to keep your looks cast down demurely. We hope that the interview will be short and thus your shame brought to an end.'

'Papa is determined to humilate us by a visit to Hartcross!' Emily had announced to Charlotte on the morning after Martha Holmes's detection by Miss Wooler. 'He means to order the cart and take us there to apologise. Now – without delay!'

Charlotte's heart had missed its beat. A bitter taste rose into her mouth. 'We must endure it then,' was all she said.

But Emily had found it harder to martyr herself to what she felt sure was Aunt Branwell's harsh decision. 'I had rather they took away pen and paper from me, and confined me in the house for an entire year than suffer this!'

'By "this" you mean the pitying gaze of Mrs Holmes and the contemptuous glance of her husband?' Charlotte had asked, steeling herself for the occasion as she stooped to tie the laces to her boots.

'Not to mention Martha's anger,' Emily had reminded her. 'I believe she will scratch out our eyes in vengeance if she finds the opportunity.'

'Ah yes, Martha, the star-crossed lover,' Charlotte had said with a touch of dry humour. 'I hope we shall not see her today at Hartcross Manor.'

She hoped so still as the cart rattled up to the wide doorway. Looking up at the two-storey building and the mock battlements on its long roof, she pictured the eyes of servants and family alike watching their arrival.

'Remember, girls – let Branwell take the lead,' Mr Brontë reminded them as he raised the heavy knocker and let it fall.

A housekeeper answered, keys hanging from her waist. Her dark green dress was trimmed with white lace at the collar, her hair was neatly parted and braided, her face impassive. 'Mrs Holmes will see you in the library, sir,' she said quietly.

Mr Brontë nodded and followed with Branwell, the girls trailing behind across a wide hall and down a long, panelled corridor with closed, oak doors to right and left. Fine Turkish rugs softened their footfall, until the housekeeper opened one of the doors and ushered them into a room lined with books, with a large, polished desk by the window.

'Your visitors, madam,' the housekeeper said, and then withdrew.

Mrs Holmes came out from behind the desk. 'Mr Brontë,' she began, with a slight, stiff bow.

'Mrs Holmes.'

Charlotte's whole frame shook with shame. Emily held her breath lest she cry out in anger. Branwell stood like a hare fixed in the glare of a hunter's torch.

'I am afraid my husband keeps to his bed and is too ill to see you this morning,' the lady went on. 'But I am grateful to you for the trouble you have put yourself to.'

'It was the least we could do, ma'am. My sister and I are sensible of the harm which Emily, Charlotte and Branwell have done. They are foolish children, Mrs Holmes, and are here to do their duty and apologise.'

Mrs Holmes nodded. 'They are partly to blame, it is true. But Martha has deceived us equally, and as yet expresses no regret.' She came forward to take Mr Brontë by the hand and ask fearfully, 'What are we to do, sir? In what way are we to blame?'

'Calm yourself,' Mr Brontë begged, taken aback by the unexpected plea. 'We must pray to God that He will show them the way of righteousness. For our own part, we must discipline the wrongdoers and beg His pardon.'

'Yes, yes, of course. You are a man of God, Mr Brontë, and you guide your children along the Christian path, I see that clearly.'

'Branwell, what do you say?' Mr Brontë prompted.

'We are extremely sorry, madam,' Branwell stuttered. 'We have been careless of your feelings and dishonest in our actions, but we have learned our lesson well.'

Charlotte gazed at the pattern on the crimson carpet, while Emily stared defiantly at the sparkling crystal drops on the large chandelier. Both felt as if they were caught in a bad dream where things were said and done beyond their control.

'I am glad of it,' Mrs Holmes said, but her outer shell of dignity and poise was crumbling before them. Her eyes were shadowed, her lips trembling. 'Oh Mr Brontë, we are in despair over Martha. We have given her a world of comfort – nay, of luxury – and she throws it in our faces. There is no gratitude, no duty, no love in her heart. And her poor papa is ill. He grieves over her – his days are fretful and feverish, his nights worse.'

'Madam,' Mr Brontë interrupted, stepping backwards and gesturing Emily, Charlotte and Branwell from the room. 'Look to your son, James for support in your time of trouble. Pray that your husband's suffering will be lifted, for we are in God's hands.'

Seeing that he was leaving, Mrs Holmes broke down completely. 'What shall I do?' she wept.

And that was how they left her – weeping and finding no comfort in Mr Brontë's stilted words.

They saw no sign of either James or Martha as they hurried from the grand house, only the housekeeper standing in the main hall to see them out, and from the outside, row upon row of blank, mullioned windows glinting in the weak winter sun.

That was Christmas of 1832, and the family had a very bad time of it through the period of festivities, as it should have been.

Master stood up in the pulpit and reminded his flock that Jesus had been born in Bethlehem in a stable, and that His coming had lit up the benighted world. But the children could see no light – only shame and bitterness.

Charlotte in particular took it hard. She left off eating, taking no more than a sparrow would at suppertime, and then nothing to break her fast in the morning, and the same again at dinner.

'At this rate, Charlotte cannot keep body and soul together,' I warned my mistress. I said she should tell master that he would soon lose another of his daughters if he did not pay heed, but she shook me off. She was on the severe side and a devil for discipline, was Miss Branwell.

As for Emily, as usual when in trouble, she looked stern and said little.

Poor Anne suffered for them both. You never knew anyone for softness and sentiment as little Miss Anne.

Branwell though went about crowing that he himself had won the heart of Miss Martha Holmes, and that from henceforth the filthy stable boy from Hartcross would stand no chance with the young lady.

I wondered then, and you must wonder too, how the boy's head came to be stuffed with such nonsense. He grew up vain and foolish and remained so until he died, though I fear master never saw it.

So, I say again, Christmas was a sorry affair, and all the time Emily was brooding while Charlotte sorely repented the part they had played thus far in the downfall of the Holmes family at Hartcross. Worse was to follow, as you shall see.

Twelve

'He's still up there, I swear!' Branwell rehearsed his swordplay in the back yard of the parsonage. It was evening, and he fought his own shadow cast onto the flags by the oil lamp at the kitchen window. It was January, frost held all Haworth in its iron grip.

Emily emerged from the house bearing a wooden scoop filled with seed for the geese who, thanks to her, had escaped the Christmas table. She crossed the yard without replying and disappeared into the outhouse amidst a flapping of wings and a loud cackling.

'I mean your hero, the stable boy!' Branwell jeered, thrusting and parrying with an invisible enemy. 'He lurks up there on the moor, living on what he can steal, waiting his chance!'

'He is not my hero,' Emily muttered, emerging to fling the empty scoop against the doorstep and glowering at her brother. Then she looked up at the stars in silence.

'Oh yes, he is your Zamorna, your love, your life!'

Emily sighed. 'He is not mine. And if you had seen

him you would not call him Zamorna, or any figure out of a made-up tale. Rather you would say he is an ordinary man driven almost out of his wits by the cruelty of his old master.'

'Ordinary? Nay, not even so much!' Determined to goad her, Branwell came and stood close. 'I just talked to Henry, who saw him two days ago while he was carting worsted cloth to Colne. Your Heslington cuts a poor figure by his account.'

Emily was startled but would not let it show. 'How so?'

'Hah! Well, let me see. Henry came through a sudden snowstorm, out onto the moortop. He says he saw what he took for a beggar by Haygarth Falls – a scarecrow in rags, sheltering under a cliff, who saw the cart too late to avoid notice. He could scarcely stagger away, he was so emaciated, but he vanished behind the falls before Henry could call out to him.'

'And was he sure it was Heslington?' Emily's heart raced in spite of herself. For weeks now she'd kept silent on the subject. *I played my part*, she'd told herself. *I kept faith with him. Now it is beyond my power.*

'Tall and spare, with black hair and a stare that would cut through you like a blade,' Branwell reported.

Emily nodded.

'Well, you may go and tell your friend, wherever he stays, that he wastes his time,' Branwell grinned. He pulled her away from the door and spoke in a whisper. 'I have written a secret letter to Martha, confessing my attachment,' he confided. 'She has replied.'

Gasping and pulling free, Emily rounded on him. 'Branwell, do not jest!'

'I am in earnest!'

She took a deep breath. 'Did her reply give you any encouragement?' she asked stonily.

Branwell lifted his head with a faint, proud smile, but he refused to elaborate other than with, 'It would be a kindness to the stable boy if you were to put him out of his misery and tell him that Miss Martha's affections have found an object more worthy of her station in life.'

Emily stared in fury at her vain and pompous brother. 'You are a fool!' she said shortly, turning on her heel, opening the kitchen door then slamming it firmly behind her.

'Mrs Collins!' Tabby announced, showing a New Year visitor into the parlour where Aunt Branwell sat with Emily, Charlotte and Anne.

The girls got up from their sewing to curtsey. Mrs Collins sat demurely in the high-backed chair closest to the fire.

'January is a cruel month,' Aunt Branwell began, noting their guest's chafed fingers and reddened cheeks.

'In my native Penzance we could ride out the winter in relative comfort, without such snows and frosts!'

Mrs Collins returned pleasantries on the weather while Charlotte, Emily and Anne took up their needles. Their heads were safely bowed over their work when the grown-up conversation took a startling turn.

'You have heard of poor Mrs Holmes's sad loss?' Mrs Collins inquired, by now furnished with hot tea in a china cup, provided by Tabby.

'No indeed,' Aunt said with an edge in her voice.

'She has lost her husband, and in the worst of circumstances.'

'Mr George Holmes is dead?'

Mrs Collins nodded. 'Two days since.'

'God rest his soul,' Aunt Branwell murmured. 'He had been ailing, had he not?'

'Aye, but there is more to it,' Mrs Collins confided. 'My dear Miss Branwell, when I say the worst of circumstances, I mean that the poor man's death may not have been entirely – well – natural!'

The girls looked up to see a deep frown on their aunt's face.

'Not natural?' Aunt echoed. 'How then?'

Mrs Collins bent forward as if to exclude the girls, but her voice remained audible in the small, airless room. 'They say that shock played its part, poor man.'

Charlotte stole a glance at Emily, whose attention was fixed on the visitor's mouth, as if she would run to catch every word before it flowed from her lips. 'You see, there was an unwelcome guest at Hartcross on Monday night,' Mrs Collins whispered. 'Nay, to be blunt, an intruder was discovered!'

Aunt Branwell clutched the tight lace collar at her throat. 'And Mr Holmes intercepted this ruffian?'

Another nod from Mrs Collins confirmed Aunt Branwell's guess. 'In the library, amongst his books. The old man had heard the noise of breaking glass, so he lit a candle and came downstairs, though he had not left his bed these four weeks or more. They say he found the man and stood up to him at first, but it was too much for his weakened frame to bear, and so he died.'

'God forbid!' Aunt gasped.

Still Charlotte stared at Emily, whose eyes reflected unconcealed horror.

'What was the intruder's name?' Emily gasped. 'Tell us, please!'

The visitor turned to her, no doubt recalling a rumour she had heard before Christmas about Emily's foolish involvement with the disgraced groom. 'It was Heslington,' she said coldly. 'The villain broke into the house with the intention of stealing all he could carry. And now George Holmes lies dead because of it.'

'I do not believe it!' Emily cried.

Charlotte had marched her and Anne out of the house into the village before she would allow them to discuss the news they had just heard. 'Calm yourself!' she insisted. 'A man is dead, and another accused. There can be no argument about the facts.'

Anne closed her eyes in prayer and stood still on the pavement.

'I do not believe the part about Heslington!'

'God forgive us all!' Anne pleaded.

But Emily wrenched at her hand. 'God has nothing to do with this, Anne! We must think, we must not be swayed by mere rumour. How is it possible that Heslington could do what he is accused of?'

'Very easily possible,' Charlotte countered, standing outside the ironmonger's shop and staring down the steep, narrow street. 'He has a motive, does he not?'

'To avenge himself against the family who thrust him out,' Anne acknowledged. 'Angry men commit violent acts.'

'Yes. Or you must consider the possibility that Heslington returned to Hartcross to gain access to Martha once more,' Emily reminded them, thinking that this explanation might convince Charlotte. 'Such a man – a man of strong feeling, as you yourself admit – would not give up the woman he loves without a struggle. And Heslington has spent many lonely months waiting for Martha Holmes to fulfil her promises. Perhaps solitude and a sense of loss drove him to this latest act! *If* it is even true!' Emily insisted.

She was the first to spy Branwell emerging from the cobbler's shop further down the main street. Their brother broke off from conversation with a lad from the lower village and sprinted up the hill towards them.

'Here's more to do!' he cried, then halted his stride. 'Ah, I see from your faces that you have heard the news!'

'Yes, and we take less joy in it than you seem to do,' Charlotte commented, alarmed to see a wild light in Branwell's grey eyes.

'Why, you know 'tis better than our plays!' he confirmed. 'And happening on our doorsteps. Here's a fine tale of greed and revenge to fire the imagination.'

Sighing and shaking her head, Emily was ready to walk away, until Anne stopped her with a question for their brother. 'Come tell us, Branwell, what is it exactly that you have heard?'

'That old man Holmes is killed!' he declared. 'The whole village is afire with it, and all the valleys far and wide.'

'Killed, you say?' Emily said. You mean by the shock of discovering the intruder?'

'Shock?' Branwell echoed. 'Why no – from what I hear 'twas more like a blow to the skull from a cudgel that did the job!'

Anne groaned and clutched at Charlotte's hand, Emily narrowed her eyes. 'Now we will hear the worst of it,' she muttered. 'Go on, Branwell, tell us.'

Their brother crouched low in the porch leading into the dark shop full of iron pots, pans, nails and hooks. He re-enacted the scene as he described it in detail. ' 'Twas the dead of night,' he began. 'Not a light in all the house to guide the dark figure making its way across the park. There was no moon. The avenue of oaks shaded the intruder's progress, until the wretch came to the library window and peered inside.'

'Please, Branwell!' Anne begged.

'He knew the house well. There had been a loose pane in one of the windows which George Holmes had meant to have repaired. The intruder's plan was to remove the pane and reach his hand inside so as to open the fastening. But he found that the old man had indeed mended the window, and so he must break the glass and run the risk of waking the house.'

'Which he did,' Charlotte cut in. 'According to Mrs Collins, Mr Holmes wakened and came downstairs.'

'Aye, worse luck for the black-hearted villain,' Branwell confirmed, miming the action of an old man descending by candlelight. He saw that he had gathered a small audience of village children, all standing round gasping and adding scared laughter to his account. 'The blackguard had scarcely climbed in through the casement when the inner door opened and George Holmes appeared, demanding who it was and what he wanted.'

With a pause for dramatic effect, Branwell showed on the one hand how the old landowner would have confronted the intruder, and then springing around to face the other way, showed a brutish villain standing full square to confront him. 'Thief!' he cried in an old man's voice. 'You are a rogue sir, to try to steal my daughter from under my nose!'

'Oh!' the girls from the village cried. And they giggled and pretended to cower away.

'And you are a bloody tyrant!' Branwell called out in a broad Yorkshire voice that he thought would represent Heslington's. 'You brought me up as a son, only to banish me. And all because your daughter saw fit to love me as more than a brother!'

'Ahh!' the children gasped.

'And now I am come to take my revenge!' Branwell went on, strutting out of the shop porch with a broad staff which he had seized from inside the doorway. He raised the stick and brought it crashing down three times. 'Take that, sir! And that, and that!'

Anne winced. The bigger children cried out, the small ones ran away.

Branwell spun around and played the helpless victim. 'Aagh!' he cried, raising his hands to shield his head.

Then he dropped to the ground, face down and lay motionless.

A slow applause broke the awed silence and John Brown stepped out of the ironmonger's shop.

'Bravely done!' he quipped, offering his hand and pulling the boy back onto his feet. 'You have it to the very life, Branwell.'

'So it is true?' Charlotte asked him, while Emily and Anne hung back.

The sexton nodded gravely. 'Heslington has killed the old man,' he confirmed. 'And now all they must do is catch the vicious cur and hang him by the neck until he is dead!'

Charlotte Bronte: *Retrospection,* written December 19th, 1835

We wove a web in childhood,
A web of sunny air,
We dug a spring in infancy
Of water pure and fair;

We sowed in youth a mustard seed,
We cut an almond rod;
We are now grown up to riper age;
Are they withered in the sod?

Are they blighted, failed and faded,
Are they mouldered back to clay?
For life is darkly shaded,
And its joys fleet fast away!

Letter from Charlotte Bronte to Ellen Nussey, January 10th 1833

Dear Ellen,

Alas, I can hardly write, I have such a dreary weight at my heart. I have been perplexed these many days over what to do about Emily, who goes about so solitary that I fear she has gone mad.

To cut to the quick – the matter concerns the recent death of a distant neighbour of ours, whose daughter you will well remember, for she was for a short while a pupil at Roe Head, and whose name is Martha Holmes.

You will recall, I suppose, that Miss Martha proclaimed herself in love with a certain groom in her father's employ, going under the singular name of Heslington, though whether this is a family name or the one by which he was baptized (if indeed this reckless individual was ever entered into the Christian church by his long absent mother and father) I cannot tell.

However, I digress. You will recall, dear Ellen, that this ill-starred love affair ended in disaster some months since with the dismissal of the groom, the sending of the girl to school, and then her recall to Hartcross.

And so the matter should have rested, and my sister Emily's shameful part as go-between for the lovers forgotten after a formal apology delivered in person, to my own great discomfort. To tell the truth, Ellen, I was stung to the heart by Emily's involvement and my own weak will to prevent it. As for Branwell, I cannot describe the foolishness of his actions without an acute sense of shame – he who once held such promise and is now a source of despair.

Well now, there have been developments, and we are as it were in the midst of a miserable dream here at Haworth. To be specific – the old man, Martha's father, has been killed in his house by an unknown intruder. There is a great hue and cry, and the word is out that the culprit is no other than – yes, Ellen, you have guessed it – the outcast, Heslington!

There is no actual proof, so far as we know, but now rumour runs amock. The search is on and suspicion casts a wide shadow. It is supposed, for instance, that Emily knows more of the whereabouts of the wicked runaway than she tells.

Now, this is a grave charge, and one which Emily herself steadfastly refuses to address. So Papa and Aunt closet themselves in the parlour and discuss the matter fervently – should Emily be forced to give an account of every walk she takes? Should she be confined to the house? Can information be forced out of her mouth by fair means or foul?

Oh, it is a dreary business, Ellen, and I wish I were back at Roe Head with you, and out of its clutches!

Emily keeps to her room, or else walks Captain on the moor in stubborn silence. Anne sighs and cannot tell what to do. Branwell, on the other hand, comes alive at the drama of the occasion. He takes every occasion to insert himself in the core of the action without any justification. Meanwhile, Aunt frets, Papa shakes his head and Tabby tries but fails to feed us all heartily, as though a solid helping of boiled beef were the cure to all ills!

All is confusion, dear Ellen. Do you have any advice? If so, send it in a letter as soon as you are able.

Forgive me for burdening you with my troubles.

I remain, as ever, your most sincere friend,

Charlotte Brontë.

Emily Jane Brontë's Diary Papers, January 11th, 1833

I fed Captain, Jasper (pheasant), Diamond and Snowflake (geese).

This morning Branwell went down to Keighley and brought news that the River Calder is frozen over in parts. Anne and I have been making more quills out of ravens' feathers. It is past twelve o'clock and I have not tidied myself, done my bed-work, or my music exercise which consists of b major.

Fine, very cold day. Aunt working in the little room. Papa gone out.

The Gondalians are at present in a threatening state, but there is still no open rupture.

I close, sending from far an exhortation, 'Courage, courage!' to an exiled and persecuted friend, hoping he will be given justice and the chance to clear his injured name.

Thirteen

The day of George Holmes's funeral dawned clear and bright.

Mr Brontë, insisting that the whole family, excluding his sister-in-law, should attend the service at Hartcross out of respect for the dead man and his widow. He made the girls and Branwell rise at five o'clock, ready for the cart to carry them over the moor, which was to arrive at the parsonage by six.

Emily and Anne dressed and ate breakfast in uneasy silence. They knew that the day would prove trying in the extreme, but they submitted to their father's will. Charlotte, however, refused Tabby's porridge and trembled as she pulled her cloak around her thin shoulders.

'Have pity, Papa!' Emily declared, indicating that her older sister was clearly unwell. 'Charlotte cannot make the journey. Let her stay behind with Aunt.'

And so Mr Brontë grudgingly released Charlotte from her duty. He went to stand sentry at the long landing window overlooking the churchyard and the street beyond, tapping the face of the clock and fretting over Henry Poole's late arrival.

'Thank you,' Charlotte said to Emily, taking off her cloak and sitting by the kitchen fire. 'I think it might have almost killed me to stand in Hartcross Church today and witness the grief of that poor widow!'

'You feel too much for others,' Emily said more gently than usual. 'But remember, Charlotte, that we know little of the real circumstances of Mr Holmes's death, and I for one refuse to believe the worst!'

Charlotte sighed. 'You still take a favourable view of our friend on the moor?'

'Hush!' Emily warned. 'Don't mention the moor, for if word gets out that he once took refuge there, then they will hound him and corner him like a stray dog!'

'Do you wish him to escape justice?'

'No. Believe me, Charlotte, I hope to see justice done, but fear that Heslington is already judged and condemned without trial!'

Charlotte shrank back under the rush of Emily's warm feeling on the runaway's behalf. 'Don't you think that we have contributed?' she murmured. 'Tell me the truth – would the situation have run so far out of control if you – or we – had not played our part?'

'If I had not carried Heslington's message, you mean?'

Emily closed her eyes and bent her head. Then she shrugged. 'What is the point of wondering about it? It is done.'

'Yes. But oh, Emily, I am afraid we have meddled too far!'

'We are not to blame. We don't rule another's passions – Heslington would have loved Martha without me acting as his messenger. But there *is* something that troubles me in all this, Charlotte, and it is that Martha does not deserve his love!'

Charlotte shook her head in exasperation.

'No, listen! She is a spoiled, petted creature, is she not? She toys with his affection, there is no constancy in her.'

'And yet he has chosen her,' Charlotte insisted. 'Even if what you say is true – that Heslington has been unfairly treated and Martha is a vain fool – who are we to judge from the outside what is felt by those to whom this affair is life and death?'

Emily took this in then nodded. 'I think I shall never truly understand affairs of the heart.'

Charlotte agreed. 'It happens differently in real life. Poetry has perhaps given us a false view.'

'Then let us blame Byron and Scott!' Emily smiled wryly.

'And you will promise not to interfere any more?' Charlotte pleaded, looking up from her seat by the fire and noticing that Tabby was coming to beckon Emily to the front of the house.

Emily regarded Charlotte with a steady, calm gaze. 'Very well, I promise,' she murmured.

After the funeral, the mourners gathered in the church porch, where they thanked the parson, the Reverend Jennings, and expressed their sympathy to the bereaved.

'Your husband gave good service to the parish,' they told Mrs Holmes. 'He was upright and honest. He was a generous benefactor to the local school.'

The widow kept her daughter and son close to her and hid her tears behind a heavily-veiled bonnet. She murmured her thanks.

Out in the graveyard, the gravediggers poured earth onto the coffin.

Watching the heavy occasion from a safe distance, and with the sound of the organ music still in her ears, Emily couldn't help but notice the expressions on the faces of James and Martha Holmes. The son held his head up and clenched his jaw so tight that muscles jerked constantly in tiny spasms. His forehead was creased in a frown that dug a deep furrow between his heavily-lidded brown eyes. The daughter, for her part, stood with her head bent and avoiding everyone's gaze, her hands clasped in front of her.

'Be assured your husband is with God,' Mr Brontë approached Mrs Holmes and spoke confidently. He talked a little more, then turned to the parson of Hartcross and shook his hand. The two men of religion withdrew to a quiet corner.

And now it was Emily, Anne and Branwell's turn to line up and murmur their remarks then pass on into the cold churchyard once more.

'We are so sorry,' Anne said simply.

'He was a brave man,' Branwell said, adding, 'He died defending his home.'

The remark caused James Holmes to turn aside with an inaudible curse. A sob escaped from Mrs Holmes, while Martha looked up for the first time.

The boldness of the girl's look struck Emily as odd. There was a hint of a smile in the curled corners of her mouth. 'Yes, my father defended his property at all costs,' she said. Then the sobbing mother drew the parson back among the mourners, and soon Mr Jennings took control.

It was while Emily, Anne and Branwell were waiting by the lychgate for their father to conclude some small business with the sexton and the curate of Hartcross that Martha Holmes sought them out.

Many of the mourners had already dispersed, and the girl carefully chose her moment to break away from her mother and brother who were still in the porch. She came down the path between the weather-worn gravestones, walking not like a girl who had suffered great loss, but with a spring in her stride and with firm purpose.

It was Branwell who stepped forward to greet her, bare-headed, with his hair swept across his forehead by the stiff breeze. 'You did not reply to my last letter!' he chided. 'Martha, how could you make me wait?'

'I have had other things on my mind,' she said coolly. 'Besides, Branwell, you presume too much!'

The rebuff threw him. 'How do I presume? Do you not value my letters?'

'I value them as I do letters from all my acquaintances – no more, no less.' Saying this, Martha turned her attention to Emily. 'When did you last see Heslington?' she asked.

But Branwell was stung into retaliation. 'Acquaintance!' he echoed. 'We are more than that, are we not? Your letters persuaded me that we were.'

Martha made it plain that Branwell had tried her patience by stepping in between him and Emily. 'I wrote them in idle moments, for my own amusement,' she told him briskly. 'Surely you did not take the silly things as more than that.'

'Indeed I did!' Branwell retorted in a wounded voice. 'For you signed them very affectionately and gave me to believe you were serious.'

'Then I am sorry to tell you plainly now that you are nothing to me and that you are yet more foolish than I first supposed.'

As Branwell faded back in dismay behind a blackened tombstone, Martha continued her questioning of Emily. 'I ask you to give me news of Heslington. Where is he? How does he? Have you had communication with him?'

Startled, Emily shook her head. 'I have heard rumours. That is all.'

'Well, we have all heard the rumours,' Martha declared. 'They make Heslington a thief and a murderer – an inhuman monster who would prey on an old man, and when he could not steal his daughter, turned instead to breaking into the house in the dead of night.'

Emily felt herself turn pale. 'I do not believe it,' she said stoutly, though she was shocked by the girl's seeming indifference.

'Do you wish to know who started this tale?' Martha demanded, casting a quick look back at the church. 'It was my brother James who raised the alarm. He went to the library on that night, too late to save my father, but soon enough to identify the attacker. And the name he spoke, first to my mother and then to the magistrate's men when they came calling, was Heslington!'

'James saw him?' Emily repeated. She too glanced

across the churchyard towards Mrs Holmes and her son.

'James *says* that he saw him,' Martha corrected. 'But my brother has long hated Heslington. It is a festering dislike. Ever since Papa first brought Heslington home and employed and educated him, James has been angry over it.'

For a while Emily didn't speak. A new picture formed in her mind of life lived on a knife's edge at Hartcross – the jealousies, the suspicions and perhaps impure motives behind the actions of the two rivals. 'You take me by surprise,' she murmured. To the stranger, Hartcross had seemed a calm and peaceful place, nestling as it did in its sheltered hollow.

'James hated Heslington from the start,' Martha insisted. 'Papa often warned him to show more charity, but James never could. He swore it was wrong to give an interloper and a mere servant the freedom that Papa afforded Heslington. And so it went on, throughout my childhood.'

For the first time Emily felt stirrings of sympathy towards Martha Holmes. She thought she saw signs of suffering behind the cool exterior. 'And then you fell in love,' she added quietly.

'Ah, love. Yes. James would beat Heslington behind Papa's back, and give him the worst and filthiest jobs, hoping to debase him further. But I took Heslington's side, and shared my books. We read in the hayloft above the stables – in secret, where James would not discover us. I did it to defy my brother at first, and for many years, but then lately – early last spring – my affections softened when I found that poor Heslington valued me more than the world.

'Because you had shown him kindness,' Anne cut in. She had stood quietly, as ever, until moved by strong feeling to interject.

Martha glanced at her and nodded. 'In another year or two all would have been well. I should have been old enough to marry in secret, and then James would have had no further hold over Heslington. Papa would have forgiven me. There is a farm with a large estate out beyond Halifax which our family owns. That would have been our home.'

'Wait!' Emily begged. The scene ran on too fast. She tried to imagine Martha betrothed to Heslington and living as a farmer's wife, but could not. 'It is James then who accuses Heslington?'

Martha nodded. 'He was the only witness to Papa's death. But as you see, his motive for naming Heslington is doubtful.'

'Surely he would not play false!' Anne exclaimed. 'It would be wicked indeed to lay blame where it is not due.'

Martha merely stared hard across the graveyard. 'I

must discover where Heslington is hiding,' she said quietly, turning her attention away from her brother and towards Emily once more. 'You have found him before, now you must do it again.'

'No!' Anne cut in. 'You cannot ask Emily. There will be danger in it now. The situation has become quite desperate.'

But Emily spoke for herself, as always. 'You ask a great deal,' she said to Martha. 'And I am by no means certain that I *can* discover him.'

'But you will try?' Martha said eagerly, making as if to end the conversation and hurry away as she saw her brother walk to fetch her.

'I will think about it,' Emily said slowly.

'No, you must not!' Anne protested. 'Charlotte says we may not interfere further.'

James Holmes was near now, and the girls' conversation became frantic.

'You must!' Martha pleaded, taking Emily's hand. 'You are my only hope. And unless you act, Heslington will be trapped and taken before the judge. He will be hanged as a thief and a murderer!'

Emily took a deep breath. 'Anne, go and talk to James,' she ordered. 'Give Martha and me a little more time.'

At first Anne shook her head, but Emily's forceful insistence made her walk forward to intercept the brother. Then Emily drew Martha under the cover of the arched gateway. 'Tell me your plan,' she prompted. 'and be quick, for there is not much time!'

Fourteen

Emily worked out her own course of action with care.

She chose the Sunday following George Holmes's funeral as the day to execute it, when most of Haworth would be at church.

'I will not teach Sunday school today,' she announced as Charlotte and Anne got dressed in their best silk dresses. 'My head aches. I will stay indoors.'

Charlotte shook out the creases in her full skirt. 'You are never ill, Emily,' she said with a hint of suspicion. 'Nothing ever ails you.'

And Anne shot her middle sister a worried glance, which was returned with a warning stare.

'I have a headache,' Emily repeated stubbornly. 'You are not the only one, Charlotte, to suffer such ills!'

'Do not repeat to Charlotte what we have heard in Hartcross churchyard,' Emily had made Anne promise on the way home from the funeral.

Anne had protested that they never kept secrets from Charlotte, and she would not start now. But Emily had argued on and extracted Anne's agreement in the end. And so the youngest girl said nothing on the Sunday morning when Emily excused herself from church.

'Stay indoors, Emily,' Papa instructed, setting his tall hat at an angle and fixing his spectacles more firmly on his nose. Then he set out into the dull, dark day to draw more wretched souls onto the path of righteousness.

Shortly afterwards, Aunt Branwell followed with Branwell, Charlotte and Anne. Then finally Tabby put on her bonnet and sallied forth with a bang of the front door.

Emily waited impatiently for the house to empty, then she put on her cloak, called Captain and left by the back way. In her pocket she carried the note secretly slipped to her by Martha Holmes.

'You will deliver it?' Martha had hissed as her brother had finally broken free from Anne and ordered his sister back to their mother's side in the church porch.

Emily had nodded and taken the paper – sealed this time. 'If it is in my power, I will,' she had vowed.

Now she smiled to herself as she stepped across the fields with the dog at her side. *Martha Holmes must have been pretty sure of me to write the letter before we met*, she thought. *Either I am a simple fool to comply, or a loyal friend to desperate lovers, and to save my life I cannot decide which!*

But the belief which drove her on over the stile and across the frost-blackened heather was that Heslington did not deserve to hang.

By mid morning Emily had reached the brow of the hill close to Timble Crag and begun to walk along the ridge towards Haygarth Falls. The wind caught in the folds of her woollen cloak and made it billow behind her, but it did not lift the leaden clouds overhead to produce even the smallest patch of blue sky. Instead, the atmosphere stayed dark and gloomy, unrelieved by movement of either animals or birds.

The lack of life made Emily uneasy. As she followed Captain's cautious track along the ridge, she tried to imagine how spring would bring golden gorse to the dead slopes, and fresh green to the stretches of dark brown bog.

'Here, Captain!' she called when he ran ahead too far.

The dog returned, pink tongue lolling. He brushed through the heather, then looked up expectantly.

'What do you see?' she asked him, stopping to scan the horizon. Haygarth Falls lay about half a mile on, but as yet she could not make out the derelict cottage.

Captain gave a sharp bark, bounded away and then ran back again.

Courage! she told herself. *I have made this journey many times. There is nothing to fear.*

In any case, she hardly thought that the fugitive

would still be there. There was a general belief abroad that Heslington had fled at last, scared off from his pursuit of Martha Holmes by the hue and cry set up after her father's death.

'He's lying low in Halifax,' the people of the town declared. 'Or he is if he has any sense.'

Halifax with its densely packed streets, its dark alleyways and huge throng of inhabitants would be the place to hide. Or further away still, in a place such as Manchester, or Liverpool with its great docks and its gateway to the world.

'Aye, he's a fool if he is still lurking around these parts,' they said. 'The game's up with the ruffian. If he prizes his life above a farthing, he will be far, far away!'

So half in hope, half in fear and doubt, Emily made progress along the ridge until she spied the lonely, roofless dwelling.

Winter had worked itself into every stone of the cottage. Frost had cracked the mortar and rain penetrated each nook and cranny, so that the broken building crumbled and dripped under the grey sky. More roof beams had fallen inside the shell of stone since Emily's last visit, and few slates remained to provide shelter to man or beast.

There is no one here, she said to herself, stepping across the pile of rubble at the threshold. But she had thought so before, and Heslington had proved her wrong.

'It is Emily Brontë!' she said out loud, pushing back the loose hood of her cloak. Her voice was deadened by the walls surrounding her. 'If you are here, show yourself!'

Captain went on ahead, sniffing at the sodden ground and turning into what had once been the kitchen.

'If you do not want to speak, give some sign that you can hear me!'

The plea fell into silence, save for Captain's busy rummaging amongst the ashes in the grate. So Emily tried one last tactic to draw the fugitive out. 'How should I deliver Martha's letter?' she implored.

Seconds slipped by, Captain raised his head and listened.

Then, in a sudden, swooping movement, Heslington dropped from a space in the dark rafters above Emily's head.

He landed twelve inches from her, bringing a cloud of dust and soot which showered over her and Captain. The dog snarled and threw himself at the ragged figure, who kicked out with his foot. Captain howled and retreated, giving Heslington time to seize his staff and beat the dog across the ribs.

'Stop!' Emily flew at the man to drag him back, but only ended by lying winded on the floor.

'This dog of yours has fangs like a tiger's!' Heslington grunted, applying the staff to Captain's back and haunches until he drove him from the room. Then he slammed the door and wedged it shut with the stick.

'If this is a trap, I'll tear you to pieces!' was Heslington's next greeting. 'Tell me you have not brought a pack of villagers with you, all baying for my blood!'

'I have not,' Emily answered, struggling to her feet.

Refusing to believe her, he ran to the narrow window and leaned out. After a full minute he seemed satisfied. 'The dog has slunk away to lick its wounds,' he reported. 'I expect it will limp down to the village, but don't expect to follow, this day at least.'

'Why not? You will not make me a prisoner here, will you?' she demanded, backing into a corner by the long wooden seat.

Heslington took a moment to study her. 'If I keep you here, it will be for your own safety, you little fool. It would be dark long before you regained the village. There are hidden wells and underground caverns where an unwary traveller may fall.'

'Let me go!' she cried, pulling the note from her pocket and flinging it at him. 'Poor Captain is hurt!'

'You will stay where you are,' he retorted, thrusting her back. Tearing at the seal, he began to read Martha's message out loud.

' "Heslington",' he began. 'See, she does not call me "Dear" or "Dearest". That is like Martha, is it not? The plain name will do. "Heslington, I have a plan to bring us together at last. Your part is to find a man – perhaps Henry Poole, the cartman – who will swear that you were in his company on the night of my father's death. You may pay him to speak for you." '

Reading slowly, Heslington, tapped the paper with his free hand and gave a brief laugh. 'Martha has an old head on young shoulders. She is not averse to bribery, as you see, and a sound judge of character to boot. I dare say Henry Poole is as likely as any man to succumb to temptation.'

Emily noted from a distance that the missive was long and written in a cramped hand.

'What else does she say?'

Heslington shrugged and read on. ' "For my own part I intend to persuade Mama that there was no intruder on that fateful night." '

Emily took a step forward. 'How can that be?'

'Listen. ". . . no intruder on that fateful night, that James has played us false and invented the story to cover up his own part in Papa's death." Ha, this is very cunning!'

'I am lost!' Emily protested. 'Does Martha mean that you did not go to Hartcross as everyone is claiming? Is she right? Were you there, or were you not?'

But Heslington backed away. 'Poor Emily Brontë!' he cried. 'I would pity you, were it not for the fact that you have not played an entirely honest part yourself in all of this. You have deceived your papa and aunt, and kept from them what you knew of my whereabouts. Now you are paying the price!'

'As a prisoner!' she said angrily. 'And all because I believed in the goodness of your love for Martha!' She had been a great fool, she realized. 'So tell me, how much of what we hear in the village is true? Were you at Hartcross, or were you not?'

The fugitive smiled at her distress. 'The answer lies close within my breast, and you shall not extract it with your foot-stamping and tears.'

Emily gave a cry of anger then ran to wrench at the staff which wedged the door closed.

Heslington prevented her with a rough thrust to one side. 'Sit by the fire!' he snarled. 'Let me read and think.'

Gasping and sobbing, she did as she was told. She saw him smile, read on, and at last fold the paper.

'Picture a new story,' Heslington said, pacing to and fro. 'Here we have a frail old man unable to sleep. He leaves his bed and descends the stairs to find what comfort he can in his books. He takes a candle into his library. The son wakes at a noise on the stairs.

'Taking great care not to disturb his mother and sister, or the housekeeper asleep in a downstairs room, he follows his father and frames a plan. Suppose the old man is so sick and feeble that the least shock would kill him? So thinks the heartless and impatient youth, whose sole intention is to put his hands as soon as may be on his father's money and large estate. He bethinks himself to creep out of the house armed with an iron bar. He approaches the library window and sees by the light of the candle that the old man's head has fallen forward and that he sleeps at last. Or is it more than sleep? Has death stolen quietly over him as he read his book? The son cannot tell. All he knows for certain is that he wants his father dead.'

'No!' Unable to restrain herself, Emily stood up and ran for the door once more, only to be thrown aside again.

'I bid you listen and imagine,' Heslington commanded roughly. 'I take it you are gifted in that direction? I thought as much – you seemed to me from the start to be a girl who lives in dreams as much as in the real world. It is a dangerous space to inhabit, is it not?

'So! The son decides to make the thing certain by smashing the bar against the window like a thief. Suppose next that the old man only sleeps. He wakes at the noise, as does the rest of the house. The old man starts up, and the shock of seeing what he supposes to be a thief at the casement does indeed produce the fatal shock to his feeble heart.

'Picture the chaos. The son withdraws, content that

he has achieved his goal. The housekeeper and servants come running, but it is too late. Their master is dead and the imagined intruder long gone.'

Heslington's tale had almost run its course before Emily found courage to interrupt again. 'Is this true? Is James the guilty one?' she begged, her mind in turmoil. Facts, which had seemed so solid and certain just five minutes since, now flew in confusion around her head.

But her tormentor refused to answer. 'How will this new story be received?' he countered. 'I think that Martha must tell it skilfully if her mama is to believe such wickedness in her son. Yes – I'm afraid it will take my beloved some time to clear my name.'

Emily sank back onto the settle. 'Do not jest,' she begged.

'Oh, I am in earnest,' he assured her. 'Never more, for my neck is at stake.'

She sighed as gradually the reality of her situation sank in; that she, Emily Brontë, had recklessly put herself into the hands of a pitiless, perhaps truly wicked man.

Heslington stood before her, his face blackened by months of neglect, his hair matted, his clothes covered in grime. He smiled now at the boldness of Martha Holmes's plan, slowing his stride and at last coming to a halt near the barred door. Then he glanced at Emily. 'You must not expect to go home to your papa until my dear Martha has woven her web,' he reminded her through scarcely moving lips. 'Your presence here may be of some value to me if events turn desperate.'

Emily saw that it was useless to argue. Murderer or not, innocent or guilty, she suspected that this man's heart, if it existed at all, was hard as the stone of Timble Crag.

Fifteen

Charlotte was the first to return home after church and discover that Emily was gone. She had walked into the empty parlour, then the kitchen, and then up the stairs to the bedrooms, growing more sure by the second that the house was empty.

'Where is Emily?' Aunt Branwell demanded, coming in soon after and hanging her bonnet from a hook by the front door. 'Has she disobeyed her papa and gone for a walk?'

'It seems so,' Charlotte replied quietly. Worry made her feel suddenly exhausted. 'Captain is not here either.'

Aunt pursed her thin lips. 'She is the least biddable of girls!' she declared with a fierce clicking of her tongue as she ascended the stairs to her room. 'At this rate she will never find a husband to tolerate her rebellious nature!'

'I expect she is walking, Aunt,' Anne said when she heard the latest development.

'When she has much to think about, she walks.'

'What has Emily to think about at present?' Charlotte asked sharply.

But Anne shook her head and made herself busy in the kitchen.

'The leg of mutton needs basting, Anne,' Tabby had called, 'and the potatoes must be turned.'

'Oho, more trouble!' was Branwell's response when he walked in on the disturbance. 'Emily's headache has vanished as if by magic and she roams free on the moor! You hear, Papa – Emily has escaped!'

Mr Brontë came into the hallway and laid down his hat and cane. As usual, the morning sermon had tired him, and after a brief period of elation, he was left feeling flat and jaded. 'This cannot be tolerated,' he muttered. 'There is an unnatural spirit of disobedience in that child, which must be knocked out of her by force, for I am afraid that my prolonged persuasion has proved unequal to the task!'

'Papa, do not say so,' Anne begged, bearing the roast meat into the dining room. 'I am sure there is a good reason behind Emily's absence.'

She spoke hastily and Charlotte saw that she was uneasy. 'Tell us what you know, Anne,' she demanded. 'Has Emily confided in you and left the rest of the family in ignorance?'

Anne's flushed face gave her away. And though she tried to deny it, Charlotte at last drew the confession out of her.

'Very well,' Anne admitted. 'Martha Holmes took

Emily to one side at the funeral and handed her a letter for Heslington.'

Mr Brontë was slow to take this in, but Branwell immediately gave a loud whoop. 'Emily plays the craven go-between yet again!' he crowed. 'Well, and I wish Miss Martha joy of the black-hearted villain, for I have washed my hands of her!'

'Be quiet, Branwell,' Mr Brontë said irritably. 'Charlotte, do you understand what is going on? If so, please enlighten me.'

Shaking from head to foot with a sense of Emily's betrayal, Charlotte obliged. 'So you see, Papa, Emily believes that the man we speak of is innocent of all crimes for which he stands accused. It seems she has gone to his aid once more.'

'A letter?' Mr Brontë repeated the one word that had recurred throughout Charlotte's explanation which he had plainly grasped. It took many more minutes for Charlotte to make clear how and where Emily might have delivered it.

'You know that the groom has been a fugitive on the moor since autumn, Papa,' Charlotte reminded him. 'Emily has refused to describe his refuge, but we know that it must be high on the exposed hillside, well beyond the reach of civilization.

'And that is where Emily has walked today?' Mr Brontë wanted to know.

'We are not certain of it, Papa!' Anne broke in.

'But we would wager a guinea on it!' Branwell cried, as Tabby came in with two dishes of steaming vegetables.

'What shall we do?' Charlotte asked, wringing her hands. 'Papa, I fear Emily has put herself in grave danger!'

'She is a headstrong fool!' came the stern reply. 'We will sit down to our dinner and eat the food that Tabby has prepared for us. After that, we will consider what action we may need to take.'

'But Papa!' Charlotte and Anne cried, in mounting terror on their sister's behalf. 'How can we eat at a time like this?'

Branwell sat and seized his knife and fork.

'Sit!' Mr Brontë told the girls. 'If your sister has chosen to disobey me and put herself in danger's way, it must be on her own head.'

So they sat down miserably to their Sunday dinner. The meat on their plates lay almost untouched, and they trembled as they listened to the scrape of Papa and Branwell's cutlery.

Mr Brontë chewed slowly and methodically, staring straight ahead. Then at last he lay down his knife and fork. 'Now, girls, you may put on your cloaks and bonnets,' he declared. 'The day draws on and we must find Emily before it grows dark.'

'Wrap your cloak around you and put up your hood,' Heslington told Emily. It was mid-afternoon and the daylight was already waning. A high wind swept across the moor, battering against what was left of the shepherd's cottage.

'Do you mean to let me go after all?' she cried, jumping to her feet. 'Oh, you will not regret it. I will tell no one where you are!'

'That you will not, for I plan to move on and take you with me,' he agreed tersely, looking round the tiny kitchen and picking up the knife from a ledge beside the fire. He found rope in a corner and stuffed it into his deep waistcoat pocket, beside the two carefully folded letters from Martha.

With a start, Emily saw for the first time that Captain had sunk his teeth into the man's arm and left three deep scarlet gashes which he had left to bleed freely. Now the blood had dried in dark streaks on the pale skin of his inner forearm. 'You will not set me free,' she realized, with a sinking feeling in her heart.

He nodded at this, striding to unbar the door. 'But we must flee this place before nightfall, so do as I tell you and prepare yourself.'

Determined to resist, she drew back behind the settle, which was the only object she could use to put a barrier between them. 'You may flee if you want, but I will not!'

He laughed then and went to fetch her, grabbing her roughly around the waist and lifting her off her feet. 'I have some strength yet,' he warned, 'despite these weary months of near starvation.'

Emily struggled uselessly as he carried her from the room.

'It is your fault that I must leave my humble home,' Heslington complained, setting her down in the yard but keeping firm hold of her arm. 'How long will it be before your fearful papa sends out a search party, I wonder?'

'Nobody knows where to look,' she vowed, holding her head up as best she could. She would not let him see her fear. 'Do you think I would betray you?'

He stared hard at her, then grunted. 'It is a passionate, proud little thing,' he muttered. 'I must thank you then for keeping your own counsel yet again. Nevertheless, we must move on.'

'Where to?' she begged, powerless to resist him. 'See how night draws in. Must we walk in the dark?'

'Aye, we must, thanks to you.' Setting off out of the yard and along the ridge away from Haygarth Falls, Heslington dragged Emily after him. 'There is a place I have found still more secret than this,' he told her. 'It is in a hidden hollow, concealed by tall cliffs, overhung by dense trees. We must walk some five miles to reach it.'

Five miles in the gathering dusk. Perhaps two hours stumbling over uneven ground, close to the hidden wells and caverns which dotted this wild landscape. Leading to a new hiding place and who knew what fresh danger?

Mr Brontë's joints were stiff. He spent too much time with his books and closeted with his parishioners to stride out easily over the wintry moor. 'Run ahead,' he told Branwell. 'Go up to the crag and tell me what you can see.'

So Branwell led the way, swishing at the heather with his long stick, imagining himself leading his troops into battle. Behind him, Charlotte struggled against the wind and Anne stumbled over her unwieldy skirt.

'I see sky and emptiness!' Branwell reported, yelling down at the others from the top of the crag. 'But no sign of Emily.'

'Come down then,' his father ordered, pausing to catch his breath. 'Charlotte, Anne – stay close. Watch your footing on this treacherous heather!'

The four searchers gathered under a small copse of rowan trees. 'How well does your sister Emily know these tracks?' Mr Brontë wanted to know. 'Might she lose her way and wander off in the wrong direction?'

Anne shook her head. 'No, Papa, she would not.'

Charlotte added that the moors were a second home to Emily.

'So she is hiding from us,' their father concluded. 'Or else she is lying injured somewhere, unable to move.'

The idea made them brace themselves to step out into the wind once more. They had not gone far this time when Branwell held his stick aloft and warned them to stop. 'I think I hear something!' he cried.

Anne, Charlotte and Mr Brontë strained their ears. 'It is the wind in the bushes,' Anne concluded.

'No – listen!' Branwell made them pay yet more attention, until they all picked up the sound of an erratic stirring amongst an expanse of heather to their left. 'Over there!' he exclaimed, no longer eager to dash ahead. Instead, he hung back while Anne and Charlotte went to investigate.

Though four years younger, Anne was more agile than her oldest sister, and so she followed the sound to its source, parting the low bushes to peer into a hollow under a rock. 'It is too dark to see,' she warned. 'It could be a fox or some such creature!'

'It is no fox!' Charlotte said, crouching low at Anne's side. She made out the form of a dog, lying on its side and panting heavily.

'Captain!' Anne gasped. 'Oh Charlotte, he is injured!'

'Papa, come!' Charlotte called, standing to beckon him and Branwell. By now it was so dark that she could scarcely see their figures stumbling down the hill towards her. 'We have found Emily's dog. He has been beaten to within an inch of his life!'

'And what of Emily? Have you found her?' Losing his footing, Mr Brontë half fell down the slope.

Charlotte reached out to save his fall. 'No, Papa, we have not,' she said wretchedly. 'But I feel something dreadful has happened to her. We must fetch help – more men with torches, a bigger search party. And we must act quickly if we are to save her!'

'Do not stumble now!' Heslington growled.

Emily had lost her footing on the dark slope. She slid and came to a halt on the very edge of a deep drop into a black pool of water.

Wrenching her back onto her feet, her captor pulled her on. 'We have reached our goal,' he told her, 'so don't swoon or give me any such girlish trouble now that we are at our journey's end.'

They had walked through the fading light into the dense night, down from Haygarth Falls, across the deserted slopes into the gentler valley where Hartcross stood, choosing secluded tracks used only by animals such as deer and foxes that lived hereabouts. They had seen not a single human soul.

Twice Emily had seized a small chance and tried to flee, but each time, Heslington caught hold of her before she had taken many steps and forced her on down the slopes, through thick copses, past fast running streams. Now she was resigned to being his prisoner – too weary to resist and ignorant of where they had come.

But after this latest fall, she realised that they were coming to a halt close to the edge of the dark pond, and that there was a small structure built under a canopy of trees, so close to the water that the inhabitants might almost step out of their door into the pond. Closer to, she saw that the building was a weaver's cottage, with a row of windows to let in light on the upper storey, and a rotting wooden wheel that had once caught water from the stream that ran into the pond. The wheel had powered a loom for weaving cloth, though no doubt its days of usefulness were long gone.

'Well?' Heslington asked, as if he were a landlord showing his tenant her new abode.

Emily shrank back from the overgrown doorway.

'What? You think that there are ghosts?' he laughed. 'Unquiet spirits wandering here? Or fairies hovering over the dark water, waiting to steal a changeling child?'

'No!' Emily said, as boldly as she was able.

'It was the home of an old weaver,' Heslington told her, pushing aside the brittle twigs and brambles that blocked their way. When he opened the door, they were met by a rush of musty, damp air, as of fungus and mould growing in cellars. 'The man has been dead these thirty years, however. Murdered, so they say!'

She cried out and tugged away.

'Killed by his own brother,' Heslington grinned. 'The brother pushed him into the pond and drowned him for the money in gold coins which he kept under the floorboards.'

Trembling now, Emily felt herself forced down a narrow passageway and up the stairs into a room where an old loom stood, decaying and covered in cobwebs. She sensed the dead man's presence in the upturned stool and a pair of gold spectacles whose lenses had been ground by a foot into the floor.

'I will not stay here!' she gasped.

But Heslington thrust her inside, locking the door and calling through it by way of a goodnight. 'Did you like my tale of the drowned weaver?' he asked with a laugh.

When there was no reply from within, he altered his tone. 'Calm yourself,' he said more quietly. 'Perhaps it is not true. Yes, 'tis an old wives' tale, told by the locals to keep out intruders like us!'

Still Emily trembled. The frame of the loom towered over her, all angles and loose, rattling parts. The spiders were busy weaving the only silken fabric that the ancient machine would ever now produce.

'Sleep!' Heslington ordered, his footsteps retreating down the stairs. 'And do not fear any interruption, for no one will find us here – not in a hundred years!'

Sixteen

Despite her exhaustion, Emily's eyes did not close until well after midnight. Instead, she alternately paced the bare floor and heaved at the handle to the casement window trying to let fresh air into the musty room. The window was sealed, however, and short of finding a hard object and breaking through a pane of glass, she saw that she would have to put up with the stale smell of mould and decay. With one last rattle of the iron hasp, she sagged forward onto the window ledge and let despair overcome her.

What would happen now, she wondered? Would Papa learn that she had disobeyed him yet again and wash his hands of her. 'Emily is no daughter of mine!' she imagined him saying in his sternest tone. 'She has chosen her own bed, and now she must lie upon it!' Would Charlotte plead on her behalf? Would Anne tell all she knew?

In any case, how would they find her, here in this out of the way place? Suppose, for instance, that poor, brave Captain were to find his way back home? Papa and the rest would seize upon him and tend his injuries, they might even set him back out on the moor when he was well enough.

'Find Emily!' they would tell him. And the faithful dog would retrace his steps to the ruined cottage by Haygarth Falls. There would be great excitement when the cottage came into view – 'Captain is taking us to her!' Anne would cry, and Branwell would forge ahead, playing the hero.

But the cottage would be empty. There would be signs of recent habitation – the pieces of crockery, the rusty spade, ashes in the grate – and that would be all. It would be as if she, Emily Jane Brontë, and the desperate fugitive, Heslington, had disappeared from the face of the earth.

So Emily let herself sob quietly there in the weaver's house, scarcely noticing the tapping of the branches at the windows from the willow trees overhanging the pond, like fingernails scratching at the dirty panes. Gradually though, the sound entered her head, together with a ghostly voice murmuring in the wind – 'This is my house. Let me in!'

With a sharp intake of breath, Emily looked up. She leaned close to the pane to see whether or not the voice was real.

'Let me in!'

Instead of answering the plea, she backed away from the window, stepping on the ancient, broken spectacles and hearing the glass crunch. *It is branches knocking against the pane, the sound of the wind!* she told herself.

'They have locked me out!' the voice continued. 'Killed me and drowned my body beneath the dark water. I cannot rest until justice is done!'

Then there was a stronger gust and the window rattled as though the glass would break.

Emily gasped and pressed herself against the wall at the far side of the narrow room.

'The window is locked!' she whispered, by now convinced that the ghost of the murdered weaver had come to call. After all, this was the time, the place for Tabby's fairies to flit and for spirits to walk – in the dead of a cold, frosty night, far out of reach of other human souls. 'I cannot let you in!' she cried.

Her voice must have roused her captor from whatever slumber he snatched in a room below, for he mounted the stairs, unbolted the door and came in. 'What ails you?' he demanded angrily.

'There is someone outside,' she sobbed, cringing from both the window and Heslington.

He laughed then and turned back. ' 'Tis the wind,' he told her. 'Remember, no one knows this place.' Then, perhaps thinking that he had better check, he went downstairs and out of the door.

Emily ran after him. Real or not, the ghost had frightened her beyond reason.

'Oh no, Miss Emily!' Heslington cried, snatching her back before she could run five paces into the dark night. 'Come with me and I will show you the willow tree knocking against your window. See, there is your supernatural spirit!'

Resisting, Emily pulled back from the edge of the pond and the gnarled trunk of the old tree that had grown higher than the house, and whose branches pressed against the stone walls. Yet she saw enough to realise that there might indeed be a natural cause behind the tapping at the pane. This calmed her a little. 'I heard a voice!' she whimpered. 'It begged me to let it enter the house!'

'The wind!' Heslington said roughly. 'That and your damned imagination. Come inside and take some rest.' So saying, he pulled her inside the house and led her back to her room, bolting the door with a loud, rasping sound of metal against wood.

Emily sank into a corner, hugging her arms about her shoulders to keep warm and stop herself from shaking. Then she put her hands over her ears to shut out the sound of the branches. Only then, the voice came from inside her head, begging to be let in once more, demanding justice.

I am feverish! she told herself, jumping up and pacing the room once more. She forced herself to face her predicament – alone with a desperate captor, cut off from her beloved sisters, without hope of rescue.

Reality struck her and brought her to a standstill by the window. And now she could see that the scratching fingers were indeed thin, bare twigs, and that there was no murdered man risen from below the black surface of the pond. The nightmare receded, replaced by stark facts.

'What will become of me?' she whispered.

There was no answer, save for the wind rustling through the dead branches, and the sound of Heslington's heavy boots pacing restlessly to and fro in the room below.

Before dawn next morning, a shot rang out across the moor, fired from an upstairs window at the parsonage.

In the outhouse the geese awoke and set up a loud cackling, but within there was no reaction.

'Rouse the girls!' Mr Brontë told Tabby, who was making fires. Having discharged his loaded shotgun, he returned it to its place against the landing wall. This was his morning routine – to empty the shot through the open window, having loaded the gun the night before as protection against any burglar foolish enough try his luck at the vicar's house. Grumbling, Tabby went off to wake Charlotte and Anne, while Mr Brontë described to Aunt Branwell the plan for the day.

'Captain is well enough today to head our little search party. He will lead us to her, have no fear.'

'Pray that she has not frozen to death out there,' Aunt Branwell murmured. Her spirits were low – like the rest of the family she had slept little since her brother-in-law had returned empty handed, save for the dog, on the previous evening.

'I have rounded up John Brown and Mr Gill, the curate from Todmorden. They are both strong, active men who will lead the way. John knows the moor as well as anyone. Trust me – today we will bring Emily safely back.'

If only Charlotte could share her father's confidence. She overheard him talking with her aunt as she passed the door, already up and dressed without Tabby's call. But no, on the contrary, Charlotte was riddled with fear, for the moor was huge and the day short. Emily might be anywhere on the ridge beyond Timble Crag – somewhere high and remote, perhaps lying at the foot of a cliff, exposed to the harsh night and even now breathing her last.

Charlotte bit her lip and hurried downstairs. There was a knock at the door – probably John Brown bringing Mr Gill with him, ready to begin the search. But when she opened the door, she saw a woman closely wrapped in cloak and hood, her face scarcely lit by the dim light in the hallway.

'Mrs Bishop.' Announcing herself hastily, the woman stepped inside without invitation. 'I am the housekeeper at Hartcross.'

Charlotte nodded, recognising the neatly parted and braided hair as the visitor drew back her hood, though not the agitated expression and restless glances that followed. On the one occasion when they had met before – at the Holmes's grand house – the housekeeper had been polite and distant, keeping to the background and fulfilling her duty without comment.

'Do you have news of my sister, Emily?' Charlotte asked, thinking that this could be the only reason that the woman had made the journey in the dark.

'No indeed,' Mrs Bishop shook her head, seemingly worried by the sounds of a household awakening upstairs. 'My mistress has sent me on other business, to ask you to help her in her hour of need.'

Charlotte readily agreed. 'There is new trouble at Hartcross?' she inquired. 'Is it to do with Martha?'

This time the housekeeper nodded. 'My mistress bade me tell you there has been a rift between Miss Martha and Mr James – a fight, you would say. I witnessed it myself, and there was anger in the air, words were spoken, things said which had been better left unsaid . . .'

Charlotte waited for the woman to compose herself. She saw that she was older than she had thought –

perhaps fifty or more, with an oval face that had once been handsome, but was now lined and drawn. The hand with which she had pushed back her cloak was still fine, unused to heavy work, with narrow, well shaped nails.

'The outcome was that Mr James swore that his sister had run mad, and she in turn accused him of a heinous crime, which I cannot name. Mrs Holmes heard it all, and I had much trouble to keep her wits about her and stop her from swooning away, poor lady.'

'What then?' Charlotte prompted, aware of Anne's appearance at the head of the stairs.

'Then – and this was yesterday afternoon, as dusk was falling – Miss Martha declared she would not stay in the house a moment longer. Mr James said she might do as she pleased, for he was about to call in the doctors to examine her and have her declared mad and so have rid of her, but if she chose to leave of her own accord, he would in no way try to stop her. Poor mistress did fall down in a faint at this, as you might imagine.'

'Yes.' Charlotte took the woman's hand and led her into the parlour. 'Mrs Bishop, this is a bad situation, but how may we help? Does your mistress wish to confide in my father? Today it would not be possible . . .'

'No, no, it's not that,' the woman broke in. 'I was sent most particularly to tell you that Miss Martha acted upon her word. She went from the house as night fell. She saddled her pony and left without a word.'

'Martha has run away?' Charlotte gasped.

There were tears in Mrs Bishop's eyes which brimmed over and coursed down her cheeks as she nodded her head. 'And Mr James says that this is proof of his sister's madness. He has called the doctor, as he threatened, and is even now making ready to take men out and find her. They are armed with guns, Miss Brontë! Mrs Holmes begged me to let you know, in case you or your sisters come across the girl.'

'She has been missing all night?' Charlotte asked. 'For heaven's sake, where do they suppose she has gone?'

There was a strained silence, during which the visitor seemed to struggle with her emotions. 'To find Heslington,' the housekeeper cried, the answer bursting from her at last. 'She has sworn to elope with him, fortune or no fortune attached. But they must not marry, Miss Brontë. Indeed, they must not!'

'You see, we are not so very unfortunate,' Mr Brontë pointed out as a large group gathered outside the parsonage.

Dawn had broken, bringing a clear day of frost and wind. The light was good, and the searchers would be able to see far into the distance once they left the town behind. But the remark was not concerning the weather. 'I mean that Mrs Holmes has more to bear than we do, and she is alone in her trouble.'

'Well, we must look out for *two* lost girls now,' John Brown acknowledged.

'Aye, two needles in a haystack, instead of one,' Aaron Cheevers grunted. The old weaver had been press-ganged into service by the sexton, along with the young curate from the nearby town and two or three other villagers who could be spared from their work.

'Mrs Holmes has her son, James, at her side,' Anne pointed out, unaware of the full story that Mrs Bishop had told Charlotte.

'And anyway, our purpose must be to find Emily,' Charlotte argued. She was anxious to set off across the field, leading the way with Anne and keeping Captain at their side. She felt sorry for Mrs Holmes and had been troubled by the distress of the housekeeper, but her main concern was her sister.

'Did you sleep last night?' Anne asked as they met the stile and squeezed through.

'Not a wink,' Charlotte confessed. She could make out Branwell striding out with the sexton and curate, armed with Papa's shotgun. Their brother had almost to run to keep up, the gun jiggling awkwardly on his shoulder. 'Lord knows who Branwell thinks he might shoot!' she shuddered.

But there was no time to persuade him to hand over the weapon – rather they must all fan out across the brown slopes, watching and waiting for the dog to pick up Emily's scent.

'Good boy, Captain,' John Brown said, urging him to forge ahead though he was still stiff from the beating he had taken. 'That dog would die in Miss Emily's service,' he commented admiringly. 'Go on, boy, find your mistress!'

The notion put courage into Charlotte and Anne, so they were able to smile at Papa and encourage him on his way. 'We have good helpers today,' Anne told him. 'And above all, Captain. He is a true friend.'

They combed the hillside – ten or more figures searching under rocky overhangs and beside streams, some with guns, others with sticks, all with eager eyes and ears.

'Here is Top Withens,' Mr Gill said, stopping at the farm to ask questions of the farmer. However, he came back with the news that Emily had not been seen.

The same answer came from two more farms, and then the search party was clear of habitation and in amongst the crumbling stone walls and lonely waterfalls of the upper slopes.

'Do you think Captain has found a scent?' Anne asked as she and Charlotte paused for breath. The dog was ahead of everyone, nose to the ground, only the white tip of his tail visible above the blackened heather.

Charlotte's breathing was laboured after the stiff climb. She looked about her and saw a weathered wooden signpost pointing the way down to Haworth and over the moor top to Oxenhope and Heptonstall beyond. Holding her side, she tried to reply. 'If he has not, I fear we are at a loss.'

'He has, I am sure of it,' Anne insisted, taking a few steps after the fast-disappearing search party and then turning to wait for Charlotte.

'You must go without me,' Charlotte told her. 'I have a stitch in my side. I will rest here and then follow.'

But Anne returned. 'I will stay,' she said quietly. And then, as Charlotte leaned against the signpost, she frowned and said in a sobbing voice. 'We have not lost Emily forever, have we?'

'Do not say so. Do not even think it!' Charlotte insisted, feeling a furious hammering inside her chest. Life without their sister was not to be contemplated. Emily was the strongest, the bravest, the most fearless of them all. Her absence would be like a flame going out, leaving them stumbling in the dark. 'No, do not think it.'

Gradually the pain in her side eased and she was able to continue.

They had walked along the track for a hundred yards

or so when a new sound broke the rush of the wind and the rustle of the heather. It was horses, approaching fast from behind, hooves thundering on the ground. Charlotte and Anne turned just in time to see the leading rider rush towards them, cloak flying.

'Step aside!' the man cried, whistling two dogs from the undergrowth and galloping on.

They obeyed, pressing themselves against a rough boulder, waiting until three other horsemen had ridden by.

'That was James Holmes and his men.' Charlotte had recognised the stern features of the widow's son. 'Nothing will halt them in their search, it seems.'

'He might have stopped to share what they have seen in the valley below,' Anne complained.

Instead, they watched the group of riders gallop on, soon to vanish over the crest of the hill.

'Come, we must catch up,' Charlotte decided.

They walked against the wind until they found another track which would provide a short-cut through a knot of thorn bushes. They took this and for a time lost sight of anything except low branches and leaning, twisted trunks.

'It is slow work on foot,' a voice said, and Martha Holmes appeared from behind a rock. She held the reins of her chestnut pony in a gloved hand, balancing on a ledge slightly above them, for all the world as if she were out on a leisurely Sunday ride. 'You lack a good horse,' she told Charlotte. 'A horse is necessary for such rough going.'

'They are looking for you!' was Anne's first remark. She pointed after the vanished horsemen.

'And will not find me,' Martha said calmly. 'You will not tell on me, will you, Charlotte?'

'Your mother sent her housekeeper to warn us,' Charlotte replied, inwardly groaning at this complication. 'They are worried almost to death by you.'

'Ah, the good Mrs Bishop!' Martha declared. 'I had thought she was my friend until lately.'

Coming down from the ledge, Martha handed the reins to Anne with an order to hold the pony steady.

'She is your friend, I'm sure,' Charlotte insisted. What now? What promise did Martha wish to extract from them, and had she no sense of the urgency of their own search?

'She was always kind to Heslington,' Martha admitted. 'She encouraged our friendship. But when passion entered the case, she quite turned against me. Why is that, I wonder?'

'In any case, they are anxious about your riding away. You must go home!' Charlotte said.

'I must find Heslington!' Martha contradicted. 'Have you news that would help me in my search?'

'None,' Anne said. 'Our sister is lost, thanks to that man. She too was his friend when all about her were his enemies. But now it seems it has been much to her cost.'

'Lost?' Martha echoed, a frown lining her face.

'Yes, her dog has been beaten and has crawled back home without her.'

'Hush!' Charlotte warned. 'All you need know is that we have half of Haworth out searching for her.'

'Oh, and you wish me to direct her back home if I should see her!' Martha scoffed. 'Well, I see we have quite different reasons for braving this wild hillside. Mine is to escape from my damnable brother, who threatens to fetch a doctor who would declare me mad and have me locked away.'

At this Anne gasped in protest. Charlotte though, had heard as much from Mrs Bishop.

'Do not looked so shocked, Anne,' Martha laughed. 'That is what they do with lunatics – they hide them behind a locked door, never to be heard of more! And that is the fate dear James has decided on for me.'

She let the news sink in, and then went on in her high-handed tone. 'All because I accused him of Papa's murder! And why was that? Because he had first accused Heslington without evidence, and it was time for me to exact my revenge!'

'Stop!' Charlotte pleaded. 'We cannot understand. We do not wish to know.'

'I underestimated my brother,' Martha continued. 'In trying to persuade Mama that he, James, and not Heslington, had frightened poor Papa to death, I forgot that James would mount a defence and that he would not stand there dumbfounded, as I had imagined.' She paused a moment, and the frown deepened. 'His defence was that I was mad!' she said in a strained, high voice.

'Come away, Anne!' Charlotte said, angrily snatching the pony's reins and flinging them at Martha. 'We will not hear such tales of murder and madness. I pity your poor mother, but we will not be involved . . .'

'If you had lived under the lash of my brother's tongue all your lives, you would know what I have suffered,' Martha told them. She let the reins fall to the ground so that her pony wandered off a little way. 'He has bullied and beaten Heslington behind Papa's back. He has tormented me with threats that I would be disinherited and he would steal away everything that was mine once Papa was dead.'

'I am sorry for it,' Charlotte conceded, listening to sounds coming from a distance, from the direction of Timble Crag.

Martha heard them too, and so ran to pick up her horse's reins. 'That is James coming this way again,' she predicted.

Sure enough, four riders reappeared on the horizon, galloping back towards them. Confusion kept Charlotte and Anne pinned to the spot, well hidden within the knot of thorns. The men rushed nearer.

'Do not give me away!' Martha cried, her face unrecognisable under a mask of fear.

And in the grip of the moment, uncertain what they should do, Charlotte and Anne stayed concealed and let the men ride by.

Seventeen

James Holmes had led the search for his missing sister for the best part of the morning. 'I will find her, never fear,' he had told his mother, who had spent the night fully clothed, sitting by candlelight at the library window, lost in her own thoughts.

'Do not be angry with her!' Mrs Holmes had pleaded. Having spent her married life in thrall to a short-tempered, strong willed husband, she had now slipped immediately and meekly under the control of her equally powerful son. 'James, she is only a child – not yet sixteen. Remember that when you discover her.'

'Yes, a child who would ruin me and bring me to the gallows!' James had muttered. 'Old enough to elope and be married, but too young to take responsibility for her foolish actions!'

'You have never agreed. Ever since you were children in the nursery together, there has been bad blood between you,' his mother had sobbed. 'Always in dispute, always tormenting me with your arguments!'

'There, there, Mama,' James had soothed, as he would

a petulant child. 'Martha will be caught and brought under control – you have my word!'

And so he had set out with two servants and a friend, Charles Sowerby, from Keighley. Sowerby was a medical man, carrying a preparation of drugs to sedate Martha, primed by James to treat the girl as a patient in need of a straitjacket and strong restraint. For several hours the riders had found nothing, however – not even the tracks of Martha's pony leaving Hartcross.

'The ground is frozen too hard to take prints,' a groom from the stable had commented. 'The lass could have gone off in any direction, and we'd be none the wiser.'

Then, on the top of the moor overlooking the village of Haworth, the mounted party had come across the foot searchers for Emily. They had exchanged news, lamented the lack of clues and then gone their separate ways.

'The parson's patience is sorely tried by his daughter's disobedience,' Sowerby commented as he trotted alongside James.

'Not half so much as mine is by Martha,' James muttered, feeling weary after a morning's hard riding.

Sowerby was curious about his young friend's dilemma. 'Tell me again – what are the signs of lunacy in your sister that would warrant strong measures?'

'Unrestrained passion,' James replied. 'She flies into a temper without warning. And she cannot see the world as others see it, but must make up her own stories, casting herself as the wronged victim of imagined crimes.'

'Ah, a fantasist,' Sowerby murmured. 'But 'tis common in girls of her age. What else?'

'More precisely, she makes wild accusations against me,' James explained, reining his horse around so that they cut back along a lower track just above Top Withens. He ordered the two servants to scour the area around the farm while he and the doctor looked down on them from a place near Timble Crag. 'She pushes the blame for my father's death onto me.'

The doctor raised his eyebrows at this. 'Does she indeed!' he exclaimed. 'I understood the culprit to be an ex-groom.'

'Aye, Heslington!' James spat the name out. 'Martha has sided with the devil and fancies herself in love with him!'

Sowerby nodded, then patted his saddle bag which carried the drugs and the jacket of restraint. 'The case sounds serious, but we are prepared,' he promised, noting that the parson's search party was about to cross their path again. 'As you say, James, Mr Brontë's troubles pale in comparison with yours.'

'I'd rather be sitting by the fire at the Black Bull than freezing my old bones on this cruel hillside!' Aaron Cheevers grumbled as John Brown and Branwell hailed James Holmes and his companion for another exchange of information. 'Not that anyone bothered to ask me what I would prefer.' The old man blew into his cold hands to warm them, then stamped his feet.

Mr Gill, the thin, stooping curate from Todmorden, agreed. 'Aye, and I'd rather be visiting the sick. But picture how the girl we are searching for must fare in the freezing cold of last night. A beast with a covering of thick fur would do well to survive.'

'Then we will stumble across a corpse, and it will end in tears and a new name on the slab in the graveyard,' Cheevers predicted. 'We will have come near to freezing, and all for nothing!'

By now, the sexton and Branwell had presented themselves at the feet of James Holmes's horse.

'We have already searched the farm down yonder!' Branwell proclaimed high-handedly. 'You may call your men back, for they are wasting their time.'

Holmes stared down at the boy, who shouldered his shotgun as if he were a soldier on parade. 'A second search will do no harm,' he grunted. 'But likewise, we have searched all along this ridge, from the Crag to the Falls.' He ignored Branwell and addressed the sexton. 'Have your men gone beyond?'

Brown shook his head. 'We take our lead from the girl's dog, but the weather is against us. The ground is frozen so hard and the wind up so high that even Captain cannot pick up a trail.'

'What lies beyond the Falls?' Holmes insisted.

'More wilderness – perhaps a broken-down shepherd's cottage or two.' John Brown shrugged his shoulders and turned to stare at the craggy horizon. 'Come, Branwell,' he decided. 'We will take Captain further along the ridge. Perhaps we may find something there.'

'Aye, do,' James encouraged.

But before the sexton could re-direct his party, Charlotte and Anne came into view.

Branwell ran to meet them. 'How slow you are!' he taunted. 'Why, even Papa keeps up better than you.'

'Branwell, you must run and tell James Holmes that we have news!' Charlotte gasped.

Hiding amongst the thorn bushes with Martha, the girls had watched James and his party gallop by. Then they had pleaded with the runaway to give herself up to her brother and so end their mother's torment, but Martha had not listened.

'I will never return home without Heslington at my side!' she had vowed. Then she had mounted her pony and set off at a gallop in the opposite direction.

Charlotte had grown immediately convinced that they should have stepped forward to show themselves to James. 'It is not too late,' she had decided. 'It is what we must do, to prevent yet more trouble for Mrs Holmes.'

And so they had set off past the signpost, taking the track towards Timble Crag, until they had seen the men talking and been met by a scornful Branwell.

'What news?' he demanded now.

'We have seen Martha!' Charlotte declared. 'James must follow her quickly!'

'Seen Martha!' Branwell echoed. 'Where? Which way did she go?' Leaving Anne to explain to an excited Branwell, Charlotte struggled on up the hill.

'Branwell, Martha is so determined!' Anne went on. 'I cannot make her out. How can she love the villain who has killed her father?'

'Aye, 'tis strange,' he agreed. 'But you know they say that love is blind. Did Martha try to win you onto her side, as she did me?'

Anne nodded. 'She had such a look on her face – a pitiful look, Branwell. But Charlotte says we must inform against her.'

Branwell laughed. 'You are soft hearted, like me, Anne! You would not betray her, would you?'

Anne shook her head.

'Well, she used me and then threw me off, as she will

you,' he declared. 'But listen, I see some glory in this for myself . . .'

Anne watched him sling his gun across his shoulder and set himself in the direction he knew Martha must have taken. 'What will you do?' she gasped.

'Why, find Miss Martha and hold her to account!' Branwell declared. 'I alone will track her down – on foot and unaided. I will be the hero, Anne!'

'You see how it feels to be hunted down like a cur!' Heslington had been out for the morning, but had returned at midday to Emily in the hidden weaver's cottage. He had seen the search parties from afar, and laughed to himself when he saw them try every direction except the right one.

Emily had remained a prisoner in the upstairs room. The old house had creaked and groaned, the willow tree had rattled at the window.

He had found food from somewhere – stale bread and the remains of cold porridge in an iron pot. Emily had been so hungry that she had taken a little of the crust.

'We must lie low and wait,' Heslington grunted as he watched her eat. 'Lord knows how many days they will search before they give you up as lost.'

She shivered, then turned away to look out of the window at the criss-crossing branches and the pond below.

'You are a burden to me now,' Heslington sighed. 'Another mouth to feed, an informer against me, should I set you free.'

'I will not say where you are!' she vowed repeatedly. 'I have not until now, and will not in times to come!'

'You will when the magistrate's men come rattling their keys and asking you questions,' he retorted. 'But when I have made my plans and secured my future, then I may consider the question of allowing you your freedom.'

She turned then and confronted him coldly. 'Do your plans include Martha? Or shall you cast her off, as she has done to you once before?'

Heslington swore. 'You know nothing of what is between us! You have seen her last letter. She makes a fine plan to discredit her brother and come running to me, does she not? Does that seem like casting me off? Is that the action of a fickle, changeable girl?'

Suddenly Emily saw Heslington, not as a fierce captor, but as a weak man hanging on the word of a shallow girl. He had not an ounce of strength – not so much as a kitten – to move out of Martha Holmes's grasp.

'You will hide here like an animal until she is ready to come to you?' she whispered in disbelief.

He swore again. 'Martha is more to me than you will ever know. If the world and all its inhabitants were to end tomorrow in a terrible catastrophe, and she were to survive, I should still be happy!'

As he said this, he turned away, almost forgetting to bolt the door in his passion. But then he paused, turned back and stared at Emily. 'I pity you,' he admitted unexpectedly. 'This does not seem fair treatment in return for your kindness.'

She held up her head and looked him in the eye. 'Keep your pity, for I have no need of it! Whatever happens, I will have made my own decisions and lived by them. I have no regrets.'

'And so I must envy you instead,' Heslington sighed, closing the door on her. 'For your clear conscience is denied to me. There is much I regret, and much in my life that I would change, had I the power. But I have not. It is as it is.'

John Brown and Aaron Cheevers, along with Mr Brontë himself, were the first ones to come across the deserted shepherd's cottage close to Haygarth Falls. While Mr Gill and the other villagers searched the cliffs behind the waterfall, and Charlotte and Anne battled to prevent Branwell from going off on a lone adventure after Martha Holmes, these three went ahead with Captain, who at last showed them the barred gate and ruined house beyond.

The sexton strode ahead with the dog, pushing

past the door and climbing over the pile of stones, discovering the kitchen with its recently used grate and discarded crockery. He soon came out again. 'They were here, but the birds have flown!' he announced. Aaron went in to see for himself, while Mr Brontë closed his eyes.

'Dear Lord,' he prayed, 'We thank You for this, and trust in You. You are our guide.'

'What now?' Brown demanded. 'I am certain that the hearth has been used, but by whom? That is the question.'

'By a man who can mend a broken spade and dig with it,' Aaron said, holding the object aloft as he too emerged from the house. 'It's my belief from the evidence we see around us that we have uncovered the hiding place of that villain, Heslington!'

'And here is where Captain led us,' Mr Brontë pointed out. 'Which suggests that Emily has been here too, and that perhaps she is even now in the clutches of the man.'

The deduction drew a grunt from Aaron and John. Then the sexton turned to Captain and bent over to fondle him. 'You've served us well, but your task is not ended. Now you must pick up another trail and lead us on!'

The dog seemed to understand. He sniffed the air and began to scout around for fresh scents.

Meanwhile, Mr Brontë called the other men to join them.

'It is a lot to ask of yon creature,' Aaron grumbled, still looking about the yard and down the hillside.

'And have you a better idea?' John demanded.

'Aye, if I put my thinking-cap on. Suppose Heslington came across Emily yesterday and she was able to deliver her message. But then when she set off for home, he prevented her.'

'Took her prisoner, you mean?'

A nod from Aaron set them all considering the possibility. The old man continued, 'He means at first to keep her captive, perched up here in his eagle's nest, keeping a lookout. But then there's the dog to deal with. He gets into a fight with it and it slips away. Heslington knows it will be back, however, and this time there'll be a handful of men like us to deal with. What does he do then?'

'He moves on,' John suggested. 'Which is why we arrive to an empty house. And why Captain must pick up a new trail.'

'Where would he go?' Mr Brontë frowned. 'Come, Aaron – with your thinking-cap on, where would this fugitive run to next?'

'Further afield,' Aaron said. 'Down into the next valley maybe, and beyond.'

So the men stood on the brow of the hill, gazing

down at the uninhabited valley. Its slopes were steep, its surface rocky and bare.

'There's no shelter there,' John Brown pointed out.

'Aye, but there's hidden hollows deep in that valley,' Aaron Cheevers told them. 'I know for a fact there's nooks and crannies hidden by the rocks, with streams and water-wheels, places where weavers – men like me – plied their trade before they moved into the villages.'

Mr Brontë listened. 'Is this true?' he asked the sexton, who nodded.

'It was the old way – to build yourself a rough house by a stream, which you dammed up to make a pond. The stream powered your loom. It was a hard, lonely life, but the men got by.'

'Then set Captain in the direction of these weavers' cottages,' Mr Brontë decided, lifting his head and showing an attitude of fresh resolution. 'It is the best hope we have, and we must follow it.'

As luck would have it, Branwell too set off in the right direction in his search for Martha Holmes. Filled to the brim with bravado, he marched jauntily down into the valley, fancying that he saw hoof-prints where there were none, and committed to stealing the glory in the day's chase.

I shall find her resting her horse by a stream, he surmised. *She will be hidden behind the trunk of an old oak, but I will spy the pony. I will fall to the ground and approach on my belly, undetected. I will spring up before her and point my gun. She may scream, but I will not be deterred from marching her back to Hartcross!*

Lost in his imaginings, he covered two or three miles without bending his mind to the actual search. Then he began to grow weary, and chose to rest against a boulder, unaware that eyes were upon him.

The silent watcher crouched amongst some trees, watching and waiting.

It was while Branwell rested that he picked up the unmistakable sound of a horse's hooves. One horse – travelling at a walk, out of sight down a narrow track towards a ford across a stream.

Branwell applied himself to this new situation. He must follow the sound, but carefully. This way, he would creep up from behind and take the traveller by surprise.

The horse walked on, apparently oblivious to being followed, allowing Branwell to gain ground until he could make out the identity of both horse and rider. It was as he had suspected, and better than he could ever realistically have hoped – he, Branwell Brontë, had found Martha Holmes!

There she sat, a picture of the perfect lady from head to toe in her grey riding habit, her neat black boots dangling beneath the hem of her skirt as she perched side-saddle down the steep hill.

For a second Branwell's heart was smitten over again. But then he recalled how she had scorned him, and he watched sullenly as she urged her reluctant pony to wade through the stream.

'Walk on, you stupid creature!' she said in a strident voice, kicking and applying her whip. 'The water is shallow. What is the matter?'

At the feel of the whip, the tired pony reared and whirled around, bringing his rider face to face with their quiet observer.

Branwell levelled his gun and aimed at Martha. 'Do not move!' he warned.

She looked down in disbelief. 'Branwell, for heaven's sake, put the gun aside. What are you doing? Did your sisters set you on my trail?'

'Do not talk!' he insisted, finding that his fingers began to tremble on the trigger. 'You must do as I say and return with me to Hartcross.'

For a moment Martha considered her course of action. Should she charge her horse at the ridiculous boy and knock him down? Or should she persuade him back onto her side with smooth words and winning ways? Yes, guile was always best.

So Martha dismounted and took a step towards him. 'Dear Branwell, I have been sorely troubled since last we met. Only put down your weapon and I will tell you all.'

'Stay back!' he warned, but already he felt himself waver.

Then, before any more could be said or done, Heslington appeared out of nowhere. He sprang from behind a rocky outcrop, seizing Branwell by the throat and thrusting the long barrel of the shotgun upwards at the very moment when fright made the boy pull the trigger. There was a loud bang, followed by a scream from Martha, as Branwell cried out and staggered back. Heslington cursed as his puny adversary fell to the ground.

'Have you killed him?' Martha gasped, her hands to her cheeks.

'No, luckily for him!' Heslington replied, picking up the shotgun and seizing her hand to drag her across the stream. 'The damned idiot merely faints from shock. Come, we must be on our way.'

'You are hurting me, Heslington,' she protested. 'Loosen your hold, for pity's sake!'

He relented and waited for her to wade through the water with her skirt dripping and dragging behind her. Meanwhile, he sent Martha's frightened pony on its way with a firm slap across its hind quarters. 'Your brother and his men are closing in,' he warned. 'I have spent the afternoon watching without being seen. Now we must retreat to a secret place I have found, where we will hide. Come, I say!'

Safely across the stream, Martha took his hand once more. 'I knew you would not fail me!' she said triumphantly.

'It has been a long winter,' he muttered, studying her smooth, fair face and gleaming grey eyes. 'And I have had precious little news to keep my spirits up. But we are together at last, and this time let no man put us asunder!'

'Together,' she said softly. Now it was she who gripped his hand and smiled as he led her towards the hidden hollow.

Eighteen

Emily saw the two lovers approach the cottage hand in hand.

'Is this the palace where we are to live!' Martha exclaimed when she saw the crumbling house with its broken water wheel and mossy walls. 'Why, Heslington, you have brought me to a poor place – meaner than any on Papa's estate.'

Her petulance only amused him. 'You know I would give you the whole world if it was in my gift. Come, this is only for a day or two, until the search is lifted. Do you think you can agree to sleep on bare boards, for my sake?'

From her upstairs window Emily watched and listened. She saw that Martha's grey gown was sodden at the hem and her fair hair beginning to come down about her shoulders in untidy tendrils. And she noted that beside his beloved Martha, Heslington looked taller and stronger than ever, and still dirtier and rougher than she had hitherto acknowledged. ''Tis the tale of *Beauty and the Beast*,' she murmured, as they passed under her window then entered the house.

'It is worse within than without!' Martha grumbled, her voice muffled, but still audible through the floorboards. 'But it is romantic, is it not?'

Heslington laughed at this. 'Aye, if you consider dust and cobwebs romantic, and you are prepared to starve for love!'

'Do not frighten me,' she complained. 'And must you always look about you so furtively? Who can see us, or hear what we say?'

'No one. Take off your boots and dry your feet. Perhaps I should have carried you through the ford – that would have been the mark of a romantic hero, would it not?'

'Oh my dear, I am so happy!' Martha sighed, changing her tune as Heslington took care of her wet garments. 'You cannot imagine what James has done. He is a brute!'

'Tell me slowly,' he begged. 'Do not overwhelm me with a rush of words. It's plain to me, though, that your little plan has misfired, else why would you run away?'

'Yes, James was too cunning,' she admitted, immediately blackening her brother's name. 'He has brought Mama under his power and twists the truth against me. Do you know – he proposes to have me certified a lunatic and locked away!'

Emily heard Heslington swear at this and guessed that he must have swept Martha into his arms. 'I will grind him into the ground!' he promised in a muffled voice. ' 'Tis one thing to beat me to within an inch of my life whenever he spied the opportunity, but quite another to threaten one hair on your precious head!'

Martha must have released herself from his embrace, because she went on calmly and clearly. 'You see what James intends by this, don't you? If I am mad, then I cannot inherit my portion of Papa's wealth. It is greed that drives him.'

'Well, we will talk more of that later,' Heslington told her, his footsteps pacing to and fro. But however he wished to change the subject, after a short while he took up the topic again. 'Martha, I am inclined to think that we must wash our hands entirely of your damnable brother. Let us turn our backs on Hartcross and make our own way in the world.'

'What do you mean?'

'Well, in the end, the money is not important. We have always known that what matters is that we can be together at last.'

'Perhaps,' she said more guardedly. Then a noise from upstairs startled her. 'What is that?'

Emily bit her lip. She had drawn breath and nodded to herself when she had heard Heslington declare his intentions to renounce Martha's money. But then she had lost her balance and knocked against the loom in her eagerness to overhear their conversation. Now she heard Heslington's step on the wooden stairs. The door flew open and she received an abrupt order to descend.

'Meet our young saviour!' he announced to Martha, thrusting Emily into the room before him. 'Emily Jane Brontë, if you please!'

Martha gave a small, fretful shake of her head. 'Yes, I know who she is – one of the plain sisters from the parsonage, the go-between.'

Emily swallowed back her retort, trying not to wilt under Martha's disdainful glance.

'I heard that you had run away,' she said coldly. 'Your sisters fear that you are dead. Little do they know that you keep house for Heslington!'

'She does not keep house!' Heslington cut in.

'You have seen Charlotte and Anne?' Emily cried.

Martha ignored her. 'Then why is she here?' she demanded, almost stamping her foot in temper. 'She was required to carry my letter, no more.'

'Aye, and run back and tell the world where I hid,' he countered.

'So you kidnapped the wretch instead?' Martha said, advancing on Emily as though she would willingly tear at her hair. 'That's a fine act, Heslington! May we not live to regret it.'

'Leave the girl alone,' he grunted. 'If you think she spoils our little idyll, I will take her back upstairs and lock her in.'

He was about to take Emily's hand and lead her out when Martha prevented him. 'Do not touch her! How can I trust you now?'

Heslington's face creased into a sneer. 'What, jealous!' he exclaimed. Then, 'You have not been here above half an hour, Martha, and already you display your quarrelsome nature!'

'And if you were a true friend, you would not find fault!' she cried, easily moved to wounded tears. 'You know my nature, Heslington, and still you chose to love me.'

'For better or worse,' he admitted. Then he went on more gently than before. 'And I do believe, Martha, that when I remove you from Hartcross and all those causes of irritation, then your temper will improve.'

'Don't talk of improvement,' she sobbed. 'As though I were less than perfect!'

'Perfection is not for us,' he said with a sigh. 'I am a servant – rough and uneducated, with a passionate nature. You are . . .'

'What!' she demanded, raising her head and gazing crossly at him.

He relented then. 'You are my own darling,' he

said in softer tones than Emily had yet heard from his lips.

The lovers embraced and she went quietly up the stairs.

The day was drawing to a close in a mist that had crept down into the hollow from the open moor top. It sealed the weaver's cottage behind a veil which it seemed no searcher would penetrate, and heralded darkness long before its time.

For an hour Emily had heard low conversation between Heslington and Martha in the room below. She had closed her ears and refused to listen, had tried to block them out of her thoughts, for now she had seen the lovers at close quarters and her unease had mounted.

She will not prove steadfast! The phrase ran through her head until it became a certainty. *She seeks romance, but Heslington offers rude reality. She will not endure an ordinary life amongst the common people.*

Downstairs, there was much discussion – mostly soft and low, occasionally rising to a volume which Emily could not ignore.

'How I wish that Papa was alive!' Martha complained. 'I know he doted on me, though he did not often show it. It was not his way to be affectionate.'

'I have seen him sit by the fireside with you at his feet, him stroking your soft hair while you read to him,'

Heslington recalled. 'The flames would light your face but keep his dark. You were held within a magic circle of light which I could never hope to enter.'

'Until James would come and spoil it with his bickering and clamour,' Martha said. 'And now my brother takes command and means to disinherit me! Oh, if only Papa had not died!'

'Hush,' he begged, as though the subject must be avoided.

Martha followed his wish for a while, then began again in childish insistence. 'Heslington, there is something I wish to know.'

'Hush!' he said again.

'No, I will speak. It is about the night when Papa . . . the night he breathed his last, and what has taken place since.'

At this Heslington must have gone away from her to a far corner of the room.

'You may walk away, but the truth is not so easily avoided,' Martha said, changing her tone.

'Do not continue!' he warned, climbing the stairs and pacing along the landing.

She followed him. 'I will have it out! You know the story that James has put about – that you were the intruder at the window, the man who brought about the shock that killed Papa?'

'Aye, and worse!' he cried. 'Did I not take a stick and

223

attack the old man? Is that not why the magistrate sends his men to hunt me down?'

'I do not believe that part for a second!' Martha protested. 'Papa was good to you. I know that you held him in your affections.'

'Then what?' Heslington demanded, bursting into Emily's room, so far beside himself that he had forgotten she was there. 'Of what do you accuse me, Martha?'

Still she pursued him, delivering a withering glance at Emily which warned her not to interfere. 'I must know if indeed you did come to Hartcross that night,' she said.

He flinched, then took a step away. It was as though someone had delivered a lash with a whip across his face. 'Is this how you show your trust in me?' he muttered.

'Did you?' Martha insisted.

He raised himself to his full height then and took a deep breath. He saw Emily behind the frame of the loom, then steeled himself to walk close to Martha. 'May this girl be my witness – I did not!' he said.

It was at the point in the day when dusk plays tricks with the eyes, making inanimate objects shimmer and shift, that the first voices were heard in the hollow.

'Have a care – your horse may stumble!'

'Give me light. There! Now we may proceed!'

Heslington was the first to hear them, springing to his feet and running to secure the outer door. 'Make no noise!' he warned Emily and Martha.

'Sowerby, tell the men to follow us close!' James Holmes yelled. 'Go, man, at a gallop!'

Martha, recognising her brother's voice, heard one horseman turn and ride away.

'Brontë, have you more torches? Make your men fan out along the slopes of the valley!' James ordered. 'Tell them to beat the bushes with their sticks. If the fugitives are hidden here, we will flush them out!'

The sound of her own family name brought Emily running to the upstairs window, until Heslington raced upstairs and pulled her away.

'Not a sound!' he warned. Then, 'It seems they have joined together in their search.'

Emily, Martha and Heslington stayed out of sight and strained every sinew to listen. More riders came galloping into the hollow – probably Sowerby with Holmes's servants. There were more shouts, growing nearer, and every now and then the glow of a flaming torch between the branches of the overhanging trees.

'They will discover us!' Martha gasped, as if all their hopes were already dashed.

'Not if we stay silent,' Heslington argued. 'The house looks deserted. The door and windows are barred.'

'We are like creatures trapped in a cage!'

'Be still!' he ordered.

But Martha flew to the window. 'Oh, I can see them!' she cried. 'There is James and his friend, Sowerby. There are men with sticks and guns!'

It was Emily who pulled her back from view, and who saw how hard she trembled. 'Be calm!' she insisted. 'They may yet pass by!'

'Ho, Sowerby, here is a cottage!' James cried, dismounting quickly and running under the willow tree. He held a torch high above his head. Its flickering light fell into the room where the fugitives hid.

'I will beat out his brains if he lays one hand on you!' Heslington swore to Martha.

James was at the door, with Sowerby at his heels. All around, the searchers were closing in.

'You must let me speak to them!' Emily decided. 'It is your only chance!'

'Speak and say what?' Heslington asked. It would not be long before they broke down the door.

'I will give myself up, and then invent a story. I will send them out of the hollow, giving you your opportunity to escape!'

He drew her out of the shadows into a patch of flickering torchlight, studied her pale face and honest gaze. 'I believe you will,' he murmured.

'Yes, go!' Martha cried, almost crazed with fear.

'Invent a story. Tell them whatever you will. Only, do not let my brother find us here!'

Nineteen

Emily acted without a thought for her own safety.

Running down the stairs, she wrenched at the bolts and flung open the door, stepping out into a circle of flaming torches.

'Hold!' a man's voice cried.

She made out figures with guns under the willow tree, saw horses tethered nearby, and then her own sisters and brother rushing towards her.

'Emily, you are safe!' Charlotte cried, throwing her arms around her and sobbing with relief.

Anne held Branwell back from dashing inside the house.

Then James Holmes took charge. 'Stand aside!' he ordered, looking suspiciously about. 'What game is this? What makes you run into the sights of half a dozen shotguns, any one of which might have killed you?'

'I was frightened by the noise!' Emily gasped. 'I was lost on the moor and took refuge in the cottage. What is happening? Why are these men here?'

'How came you to be lost?' Charlotte stammered in confusion. Her sister knew every track across the moor.

Holmes ordered his men to lower their weapons. He strode towards Emily and thrust Charlotte aside.

It was then that Mr Brontë and the curate, Mr Gill, at last caught up with the search parties. They had entered the hollow to find the torches blazing in a ring around the parson's daughters, with James Holmes asking angry questions.

'What brought you here? Have you seen the scoundrel, Heslington and my sister, Martha? Speak, girl!'

'Mr Holmes!' Mr Brontë stepped forward, his face stern and strained. 'Emily is a foolish girl, but she is no criminal. You see she is distressed. Show some compassion, I beg you!'

His voice broke down her show of defiance. 'Papa!' she cried, pulling away from, Charlotte and running to him.

'Remain silent,' he told her, walking past Sowerby and the servants from Hartcross. 'I find that the Lord has seen fit to restore Emily to us,' he said calmly, 'and I thank you, sir, for your part in her discovery.'

'The Lord be damned!' Holmes cut in with a blasphemy which shook Mr Brontë to his core. 'Your daughter came running from this house into our sights – she was almost killed!'

'I *have* seen Martha!' It was Emily's turn to shock.

Though her story was unrehearsed, she spoke out to give the fugitives time to escape. 'Do you wish to know where and when? It was on the moor top, by the sign-post, this afternoon. She rode her pony towards Oxenhope. 'Tis true, I swear!'

The confession drew a general gasp and made Sowerby approach Holmes. 'That is far from here, back the way we came, is it not?'

Holmes nodded, but continued to cast a suspicious gaze around the hollow. Emily held her breath as he took two paces towards the door of the cottage.

'I fear we must give up the search for the night,' the doctor said. 'These men are tired, James. The night is too dark for us to continue.'

'Hush!' James Holmes made the men listen to the rustling of the dry willow branches and the running of the stream. The water wheel creaked and dripped.

'Martha made her way to Oxenhope!' Emily insisted, feeling Charlotte and Anne slide their hands into hers.

' 'Tis true – we saw her too,' Anne vowed.

'With the villain, Heslington?' Branwell demanded.

'No, she was alone.' Emily calculated that she had so far gained the runaways about five minutes' breathing space. Perhaps Heslington had managed meanwhile to unfasten the upstairs window and climb out with Martha. It was possible that even now they were creeping away unseen.

But James Holmes's suspicious mind would not let him leave without further investigation. 'This girl is in league with the villain!' he grunted. 'She has carried letters, and now she lies to throw us off the track!'

Saying this, he ordered the two servants to approach the door and stand guard. He sent Aaron Cheevers and John Brown to the back of the house, then made sure there was no exit to the side overlooking the pond.

'Stop him, Papa!' Emily pleaded. Her story had been too transparent. She had failed to convince Martha's brother.

'Come away,' Mr Brontë insisted, trying to wash his hands of further developments.

'Charlotte, Anne – bring Emily. Branwell, take Mr Gill's torch and lead us out of here!'

'You will follow me inside,' Holmes ordered Sowerby.

Both were armed. James was dead set on entering the house.

But as his footsteps sounded in the hallway, there was the noise of breaking glass from upstairs and the wrenching of a window frame from its hinges. The frame descended with a splash into the black water below.

James swore and raced with Sowerby up the stairs. 'We have found our fugitives!' he cried.

The searchers all came running to the side of the house which overlooked the pond. They held their torches high and saw Heslington appear at the window, then climb down onto the top of the rotten water wheel, which rocked, then steadied.

'Come!' Heslington urged, almost losing his footing on the moss-covered board, then raising his hand for Martha to catch hold. She too climbed through the broken window and had one foot on the wheel when her brother rushed up from behind and wrenched her inside. Martha fell back and disappeared from view.

Then James himself appeared in the gap, using the butt of his shotgun to swipe at Heslington in an attempt to send him toppling from the wheel. Heslington leaned away just in time. So James jabbed and swiped again, almost overbalancing and allowing his adversary to grasp the gun and tear it from him. Heslington flung the gun into the water. Then he seized his enemy and dragged him through the window, so that both youths stood for a moment on the upper arc of the wheel, struggling for their balance, then slipping and plunging through the dark into the pond.

There was a cry. One of the searchers raised his gun and fired. Sowerby rushed back out of the house with Martha in his grasp.

For a moment there was silence. The two adversaries had dropped out of sight.

Soon one head appeared, then the broad shoulders of Heslington as he struck out towards the bank.

'Where is the other? Where is James?' Sowerby yelled, letting go of his captive and running to the reed-strewn border of the pond. 'Good God, the boy is drowning! Dive in, you there, and rescue him!'

The two servants from Hartcross took off their greatcoats and jumped in. A full minute had passed by, and still James Holmes had not come to the surface.

Meanwhile, Heslington reached the bank and hauled himself out of the water. Like an enraged creature, he dashed away the helping hand of John Brown, and instead grabbed the sexton's gun. 'Stand back!' he ordered, shaking himself like a dog and aiming the gun at Brown. 'Martha, bring me a horse!'

With the runaway aiming a shotgun at the sexton's head, no one dared move while Martha untethered Sowerby's grey mare.

By this time, Sowerby was tearing off his own coat, preparing to dive into the pond. 'My God, the water is choked with weeds. Perhaps James is trapped underwater, entangled somehow!'

One after the other, the two servants resurfaced empty-handed, then dived again. Meanwhile, Heslington backed himself and Martha towards the mare, then with one swift, smooth move, lowered the gun and raised her into the saddle.

The searchers saw that his guard was down. They raised their own guns and aimed at Heslington.

'Hold your fire!' Mr Brontë warned, seeing that Martha too was in their sights.

At the moment when one of the servants at last dragged James Holmes to the surface, Heslington leaped onto the horse. He clasped Martha around the waist with one hand, and with the other took up the reins. With one swift kick and a guttural cry, he set the mare off at a gallop.

Emily and Charlotte had to step to one side. They felt the rush of the horse, saw Martha's face delirious with fear and Heslington wearing the expression of a man possessed. His eyes glared into the darkness, his arm held Martha in a grip of iron. *That is the last I will see of him*, Emily thought. *Whatever the outcome – no matter who lives or dies – I will never see him more!*

Twenty

It was to nearby Hartcross Manor that the exhausted search parties made their way that night.

Sowerby had used his medical skills, not in restraining Martha as expected, but in resuscitating James, who had been dragged out of the pond unconscious and almost frozen to death. His wet clothes had been stripped from him and dry ones wrapped around him. Then the doctor had administered strong spirits by mouth and waited impatiently for Holmes to recover. All had watched the patient's deathly pale face recover its colour, until at last his eyes had opened. He had lain on the ground, too weak to move, however, and it was John Brown who had helped Sowerby lift him onto his horse, where he hung lifeless in the saddle for the journey home.

James's mother had been sitting at the window with the housekeeper when they had returned. The anxious women had overseen the patient's transfer to a warm bed, while the straggling party of men, together with the girls and Branwell, had been taken to the kitchen and given bread and meat.

'James will suffer no ill effects,' Sowerby promised Mrs Holmes. 'He is young and has a strong constitution. Keep him warm and well fed, and within the week he will be himself again.'

No one slept that night, though Mrs Bishop made beds for Charlotte, Emily and Anne, and Mr Brontë insisted that they lie in them.

'Branwell and I shall be in the room next door,' he informed them. 'In the morning, we will speak with Mrs Holmes and then take our leave.'

Emily lay down with a sore heart. Recent events kept a strong hold, forcing themselves into her consciousness – the sight of the two youths plunging into the pond, the notion that James Holmes might have drowned amongst the mud and weeds, but most of all the vision of Heslington and Martha riding away into the night. So she stared up at the white ceiling of the strange room, listening to the floorboards shift and creak.

'Emily, are you asleep?' Charlotte whispered, well before dawn. A small movement in the bed next to hers had told her that she was not.

'I cannot,' Emily confessed.

'Oh Emily, we feared we had lost you.'

'You are not angry, Charlotte?'

'Somewhat, at first – when we came back from church. But fear soon overrode anger. Anne and I thought we might never see you again, and that was too dreadful to contemplate.'

'Well, you would be rid of a great nuisance if I were to have frozen on the moor,' Emily muttered without self-pity. 'My dears, I have heard wild words in that weaver's cottage, and I have been more frightened than you can imagine.'

'By Heslington?' Anne murmured, wide awake like her sisters, and shocked that Emily had confessed her fear.

Emily sighed. 'Aye. He is like a force of nature – a fierce wind that knocks down all in its path and does not know its own power. And yet there were glimpses, for all that, of a man in torment.'

'You feared him and yet pitied him?' Charlotte whispered. 'You did not think him mad?'

'Desperate rather. When he is cornered, he lashes out.' She remembered his eyes – keen as a bird of prey. And she felt a curious sense of pride that she had known this man, and that he had revealed his innermost felings to her. Then sorrow that he had flown forever from her life.

'Oh, Emily,' Charlotte murmured.

The sigh drew Emily's thoughts back to the dim, quiet room and to the sisters she loved. 'Forgive me,

Charlotte and Anne too, for the misery you have endured.'

'We forgive you!' they whispered whole-heartedly.

'We would not have wished to live without you,' Anne confessed. 'And what would have become of Gondal? Our characters must all have perished!'

Emily smiled then. 'You would have carried on and made them live!' she insisted. Then, 'Tomorrow we will write another chapter, Anne. And Charlotte, you and Branwell will begin a fresh adventure of your own in Verdopolis.'

'We will look ahead,' Charlotte agreed. 'All will be perfectly ordinary – we will live our days in peace and harmony. Only there is the meeting with Mrs Holmes to be got through first.'

'Leave nothing out!' Papa insisted, putting Emily in front of the widow as if presenting her to a firing-squad. 'You owe Mrs Holmes the truth, the whole truth and nothing but the truth, so help you God!'

Mrs Holmes sat in a large drawing room overlooking the park. The room had long windows with crimson curtains trimmed with gold. Pictures in gilt frames hung on the walls, of men in antique costumes and beautiful women in white wigs and silken dresses. Standing beside her was the composed, expressionless figure of the housekeeper, Mrs Bishop.

'Martha has gone willingly with Heslington,' Emily began. 'She has not been taken against her will.'

Mrs Holmes nodded. 'I understand that she believes herself in love.'

'His feeling for her is sincere.'

'He is not driven by greed and revenge, as they are saying?'

'No, ma'am. I heard him say that he would give up all claim on the money. He believes they should make their own way in the world.'

'James will be glad of it,' Mrs Holmes sighed, half turning to Mr Brontë who stood to one side. 'My husband has left a will, of course. There are several legal matters to be cleared up before it can be read. But it will aid my son's recovery to learn that Heslington makes no claim.'

'What claim could he have?' Mr Brontë remonstrated. 'He was a mere servant here, after all.'

'Something more than that to my husband at one time, Mr Brontë,' the widow sighed, while the housekeeper clasped her hands more firmly together. 'George insisted on having the boy educated. Sometimes he came into the house and ate with us and kept us company. However, that day is past. My husband is in his grave, and we will never be the same.' She looked back at Emily and bade her continue.

'Heslington has waited many months and endured much hardship,' she reported.

'You pity him?' Mrs Holmes asked more sharply, her reddened eyes coming into focus and studying Emily more closely.

'No, ma'am. Yes. I do not know.'

'You believe he is in the right?'

Emily frowned. 'I am convinced of his love for Martha.' Still she trusted in the power of that emotion to overcome all obstacles.

Mrs Holmes took a deep breath and directed her gaze out of the window. 'Then, despite what James says, and despite Martha's youth, all may yet be well.'

The ordeal was over. Mr Brontë stayed in the drawing room for some quiet words with Mrs Holmes while Mrs Bishop took the girls and Branwell down the long corridor leading to the wide front doors. The housekeeper then instructed Charlotte and Anne to fetch their cloaks from the kitchen, where they had been drying overnight, and sent Branwell to the stable-yard to order the carriage that was to take them home to Haworth.

'Stay!' Mrs Bishop bade Emily. The effort to appear calm beside her mistress had left her short of breath and pale. 'Is there anything that you have kept back?' she pleaded, once Emily and she were alone. 'What is your opinion – will Heslington and Martha make a life together? Will they marry?'

Emily shook her head. She imagined that Mrs Bishop's concern lay with Martha, and the scandal that was likely to arise from her running off with the groom. 'I cannot tell, though I am sure he intends it.'

'Aah!' Mrs Bishop sighed, her forehead creased, her lips trembling. 'Where will they go? How can we prevent it?'

'I do not know where they will travel!' Emily insisted. The image of the galloping horse carrying Heslington and Martha into the darkness filled her mind. 'And I do not think it can be prevented!'

Her reply brought another cry from Mrs Bishop. 'Then God help us!' she sobbed, before Mr Brontë came striding along the corridor to usher Emily out into the carriage.

Twenty-one

'And they say that she fled with a bag full of jewels – rubies and emeralds – and golden guineas, enough to buy a passage to the New World for both her and Heslington!' Sally's breathless report filled the kitchen at the parsonage.

Tabby tutted and stirred the pot of stewed rabbit. 'They will say anything, whoever they are. But *they* would be better minding their own business and letting other folk get on with their work.'

Charlotte agreed. She took a tray of loaves from the oven and rattled it down on the table. 'People should have respect for Mrs Holmes's grief,' she advised. 'She has lost a husband and a daughter within a short space of time.'

'Aye, but she kept the son,' Sally said coolly. 'Anne, you saw James Holmes dragged half dead from the pond the night before last, did you not? Was his face blue? Had you given him up for dead?'

Anne shuddered. A whole morning travelling back in the Holmes's carriage from Hartcross, and then a night of sound sleep had scarcely lessened the horror of those events.

'Leave the child be,' Tabby scolded. 'And Emily, don't just stand there. Fetch me a spoonful of salt for this stew.'

Emily brought salt and threw it in the pot.

But Sally was irrepressible. 'Emily, you spent a lonely night with the villain, Heslington. Weren't you afeared he would thrust a knife through your heart while you slept?'

Emily flashed her an angry look but said nothing.

'It is past,' Charlotte said, tipping the loaves from their tins. She tapped the bottom of each one with her knuckles, then set it down on a wire tray. 'Go away, Sally!'

'You have flour on your nose!' the girl cried, teasing Charlotte before sidling up to Emily. 'Is he handsome, though? I heard from Jessie Fowler in the kitchens at Hartcross that he has demon's eyes, and a way of looking that would knock you flat!'

'No more!' Emily said wearily.

'At any rate, they have reached Lancaster!' Sally declared, darting round the table and choosing Anne to confide in. 'They have! I heard it on good authority from John Brown, who got it from Henry Poole. They travelled by the packhorse road – Henry swears 'tis true!'

The girl went on delivering her tidbits with a wide grin until Aunt Branwell appeared at the kitchen door and she beat a hasty retreat.

'Mrs Collins comes to visit this afternoon,' Aunt reminded Tabby. 'We will have shortbread with our tea.'

This set Tabby grumbling about the extra baking, and so Anne and Charlotte retreated upstairs, while Emily went with Captain up the field, until, sometime later, she was intercepted once more by an eager Sally.

'No more, please!' Emily begged. Like Charlotte, she longed with her whole heart to return to her old routine.

Sally dodged in front of her. 'Listen! There's a woman from Hartcross at the Black Bull, at her wits' end. She wants to speak with you.'

'What woman?'

'She won't say her name, but only asks after you and how she can find you and get you alone. I said I would come and fetch you.'

Emily felt her stomach lurch. There was only one person from Hartcross who would seek her out thus. 'Is she a woman with fair hair, neatly parted. Does she wear a green dress?'

Sally nodded, glad that Emily now seemed willing to follow her to the inn, across the field and down a narrow alleyway between two rows of cottages. 'You know her then?'

Sending Captain off home, Emily nodded. She felt hemmed in by the walls to either side, dreading the interview. Then, when she saw Mrs Bishop at the corner, she almost turned away.

But the housekeeper spied Emily and hurried up the lane to meet her. She gave Sally a penny from her purse and quickly sent her on her way. 'It has been two days now. What news of the runaways?' she begged Emily.

'No news.'

'But you must have heard – more at least than I have heard at Hartcross. James forbids all mention of his sister's name. He had a boy flogged for referring to Heslington. We are all in the dark!'

'There is no certain news,' Emily insisted. 'We hear gossip. That is all.'

'No letter? No word from him?' Mrs Bishop clung to Emily's arm as if she would squeeze information from her. 'You have carried messages between them. It is to you that they would return for help!'

'They have not. And I would not do any more. Besides, I truly believe that Heslington will persuade Martha to be rid of her family.'

'No!' The idea made Mrs Bishop drop her head and sob. 'She would not! Think of her mother!'

'Perhaps not. In the long run she may return to claim her inheritance,' Emily conceded, allowing the doubt she felt over Martha's nature to emerge. 'But remember, Martha and Heslington have each other now.'

Frowning and detaching herself, Emily stood back. She couldn't make out why the housekeeper was so beside herself with grief. Barehaded, with only a shawl wrapped around her shoulders, she leaned against the blackened wall and cried.

'They have each other, but it should not be!' the woman cried. 'I should never have encouraged it! And it is all come to this!'

'How so? What has happened?'

Struggling for control, Mrs Bishop raised her head. 'I am dismissed from my position. Mrs Holmes has turned me out of my home.'

'But why?'

'I have told her something I ought not to have done. It was a secret which I kept almost twenty years! A secret which I should have carried to my grave. But 'tis out. Oh, 'tis out!'

'In heaven's name!' Emily exclaimed, her mind whirling.

Taking Mrs Bishop by the arm, she led her up the lane, away from the town. She felt her chest pressed by a dreadful foreboding. 'There,' she murmured once they had gained the open countryside. 'I fear you are upset because Mrs Holmes has turned you out. Things will seem much better once you have found a new position.'

'I encouraged the friendship!' Mrs Bishop said with a distracted shake of her head. 'It warmed my heart to see how the master took to Heslington when he could have cast him out, as many would have.

'And when Martha came along two or three years later, she was a bonny child with fair curls like an angel. Heslington adored her from the start. I saw it and smiled, watching the two little things play, not thinking how it would end!'

Emily walked on, then waited. 'The secret you told – it concerned Heslington?' she guessed.

The housekeeper nodded. 'A year ago, I began to fear,' she confessed. 'I would see Heslington casting Martha a look, and her returning it with a little, sly smile and a pretty shake of her curls.

'They stole time to be together, feigning an interest in a book or taking a walk in the park. James saw it too, and began to be more jealous than ever. But Mr and Mrs Holmes – they never suspected, until I went to him and alerted him, and then, poor man, he was as helpless as I was to put a stop to it all!'

'But the secret?' Emily broke in. 'You must tell me!'

'It has gone beyond everything I feared,' Mrs Bishop cried. 'I have prayed and I have fought to put a stop to it, but they have eloped and we are in everlasting hell!'

'The secret! What did you tell Mrs Holmes?'

'That I am Heslington's mother,' the housekeeper answered, quietly now. Each word fell with a heavy rhythm like blows on Emily's heart. 'That George Holmes is his father. I bore my master a son out of wedlock. Last night I told my mistress the truth, and it broke her heart.'

Charlotte and Anne found Emily walking by the lower falls.

'Aunt says we must fetch you home,' Anne explained. 'Captain returned without you. She grew anxious.'

'I am here, I am well, am I not?' Emily retorted. 'You may tell Aunt that I have come to no harm.'

'But she wishes us to receive Mrs Collins for tea,' Anne insisted. 'We may not go back without you.'

Charlotte saw that Emily's renewed desire to be alone signified a deep trouble. Something had occurred which she, Charlotte, could not understand, 'Come home,' she pleaded. 'Remember, Emily, there is nothing now that you cannot share with Anne and me.'

'Hah!' Emily cried bitterly. This one piece of news had shattered the pattern of all that had gone before. She had learned a vital fact which she could never share.

Charlotte felt the force of her rebuff. She foresaw that Emily would take this fresh secret to her grave. 'Besides, the frost bites sharply,' she stammered. 'You look frozen almost to death!'

Emily turned to face the high horizon and the jagged outline of Timble Crag. The housekeeper's confession had blown like a strong gale through an autumn wood, raising ideas like dead leaves and whipping them through the air. She tried to catch at them and settle them in her mind, but each time the wind took fresh hold.

'Come home, Emily,' Anne said softly.

'Miss Branwell, I venture to say that we have never seen the likes of it in this neighbourhood!' Mrs Collins declared, setting her cup in her saucer. 'I had thought until now that we were a comfortable little community, wrapped around by these safe hills, minding our own business. Now I find that there is wildness among us, and events run out of control!'

Aunt Branwell sat in her frilled cap, her face pinched and stiff. 'May the good Lord preserve us,' she muttered, intending to discourage her visitor.

But Branwell ran on eagerly. 'Behind those stone walls lurk dark secrets!' he cried. 'We had a grand adventure, did we not, Charlotte? We hunted the fugitives by torchlight, we brandished our weapons. Why, 'tis a wonder no one was killed!'

Mrs Collins's cup rattled in its saucer as she leaned towards her hostess eager to engage in further gossip. 'They say the housekeeper has deserted Mrs Holmes in her hour of need! The woman is gone from the district without a by-your-leave!'

Emily grimaced, stood up and went to the window. Charlotte and Anne looked anxiously after her.

'The servants are leaving, the son is almost drowned, the daughter is run away with a fiend!' Mrs Collins exclaimed. 'It makes one count one's blessings, does it not, Miss Branwell?'

'To be sure, Mrs Collins,' Aunt replied, indicating with a cross expression at Charlotte that Emily's stance at the window was ill mannered.

Charlotte went to draw her sister back into the circle around the parlour fire.

'And now we hear that the runaways head for the coast,' the visitor confided. 'They were seen yesterday at a coaching inn near Keighley – a rough-looking man dressed almost in rags, with dark locks down to his shoulders, accompanied by a pretty young girl in a grey riding habit. 'Tis unmistakable.'

'Not Lancaster?' Charlotte asked with a frown, remembering Sally's account.

'No, they have travelled east,' Mrs Collins insisted.

Despite her show of indifference, the information made Emily's heart beat faster. 'Were they taken?' she asked fearfully.

Mrs Collins shook her head. 'The report reached Hartcross too late to apprehend them. A coach came by and carried them to Scarborough. They are at liberty still.'

That night Emily lived every jolt of the carriage that had taken Heslington and Martha to freedom.

She pictured the desolate, frozen hillsides beyond the carriage window, the softening of the landscape as they travelled east, until eventually they had come to the cliffs and headlands jutting out into the North Sea. There would be waves swelling and crashing onto a pebble beach with a mighty roar.

The lovers would step out of the coach to a new life, safe from the awful secret that Mrs Bishop had spilled, yet cursed by it.

Emily stood by the bedroom window, watching in agony as the clouds scudded across the face of the moon.

'They are not in Scarborough!' Branwell reported next day. He carried the news like a boy with a shiny sixpence. 'Charlotte, Emily, Anne, do you hear me?'

He came from the village while the girls were drawing and writing at the kitchen table. It was early in the afternoon on a dull, heavy day that had never grown quite light. The clouds threatened snow before nightfall.

'Girls, put down your pens!' Branwell cried. 'The most unlikely event has taken place!'

'What now?' Charlotte sighed, looking up over the rim of her spectacles.

Emily experienced more wringing of her tightly squeezed heart.

'Are they married?' Anne asked, still innocently wishing for a happy outcome.

'No, not married,' Branwell crowed. 'Quite the opposite! I have just seen Henry Poole. He has been by Hartcross, and guess what – Miss Martha has returned to the fold!'

'She could not endure a life of poverty,' was Sally Mosley's verdict. 'When she saw she must redden those pretty white hands with rough work, and live a common life, why she cried for her mama and went running home!'

Time had proved Branwell's tale true. A week had passed, and now reports of the runaway's return came thick and fast. Two days earlier, Mrs Holmes had accepted a visit from her neighbour, Mrs Collins, and was pleased to report that Martha had come to no harm. The girl had returned to her senses and disaster had been averted. She was much chastened by her experience and had vowed never to see or communicate with Heslington again. Mrs Collins duly passed on the news to Aunt Branwell.

'I will write a letter of comfort and reassurance to

Mrs Holmes!' Mr Brontë decided. 'I think it would be a fitting end to our part in the affair, would it not?'

Aunt Branwell agreed, and forbade forthwith all mention of the Holmes family within the walls of the parsonage. 'You see what happens when passions run wild,' she warned, with a piercing glance in Emily's direction.

'Are you glad?' Anne asked Charlotte after Aunt had gone to her room.

'Scarcely that,' Charlotte replied. 'It ends with a whimper, does it not? But I am not surprised by Martha Holmes's conduct. Her motives for loving Heslington were not pure, but driven by her anger against James.'

'And you, Emily?' Anne ventured.

'I will pass no judgment,' Emily declared, burying her head in the tiny Gondal script resting on the table before her. Martha Holmes had abandoned Heslington and was home at Hartcross – that fact at least was established.

'I feel pity for Heslington, I confess,' Charlotte murmured, putting down her own pen and giving way to a rare moment of idleness. She pursued in her mind's eye the image of a lonely figure shattered by betrayal, forever an outcast. 'After all, he was sadly let down.'

Anne nodded her agreement.

But Emily shook her head. 'Keep your pity,' she argued fervently, looking up and out at the moors. 'He is proud, and would laugh and dash your sympathy back in your faces.'

'You will always defend him,' Charlotte sighed.

'I will,' Emily acknowledged. She felt sure of what she said. 'Heslington is a rare being that will endure every hardship. I believe that wherever he is now, whatever he does, his spirit is unbroken.'

Emily Jane Bronte's Diary Paper,
January 25th, 1833

Since my last entry, the following events have taken place.

Martha H is returned to Hartcross after a short flight to Scarborough. Of Heslington there is no news, but much speculation. Branwell says he has gone to be a soldier. Sally says, to sail to the New World more like. We do not expect him back.

In any event, he is alone.

Martha proved to be fickle, for which I am glad. Little did she know, but her shallow nature saved them both in the end.

Now she will inherit half her papa's wealth, in spite of James, for her mama will hear no further talk of doctors. Martha will no doubt marry into the family of a neighbouring landowner.

What of Heslington in five years' time? I trust he will be in good health and earning his livelihood, as must we be here. May it prove so.

I intend sticking firm by him when Charlotte and Anne draw me into conversation. And, however they persuade me, I will not give away Mrs B's secret.

How little we know what we are.

How less what we may be.

Mrs Collins has told Aunt of another situation for

Charlotte. There is hope that Branwell will pursue his studies and one day make something of himself at the Royal Academy. He is to go on his first long journey by himself, to Leeds, to meet an artist, Mr R.

Anne and I must expect to follow in Charlotte's steady footsteps.

The Gondals flourish bright as ever. I have a good many books on hand, but am sorry to say that as usual I make small progress with any. However, I have just made a new regularity paper, and I mean to do great things!

On Friday morning, in cold, clear weather, I walked with Captain to Haygarth Falls. The cottage lies deserted and in ruins. The gate was broken and sheep were in the yard. I found a broken cup.

There was a boy by the Falls, crying that he had lost his way on the packhorse route and that a fairy had frightened him. His father came and scolded him and took him away. I stayed a while and could well imagine a spirit inhabiting that place, but it was too sad to think of Heslington wandering there, so I came away.

I have begun a poem which I will dedicate to H:

I'm happiest when most away
I can bear my soul from its home of clay –

And so I close my paper.

Tabitha Ackroyd's account, summer 1854

I cannot now recall the name of the housekeeper at Hartcross. I am 83 years old and my memory is not what it was.

You ask about the Holmes family – well, you may travel there in half a day and find out for yourself how Mr James runs the estate since his mother died. I have nothing to do with the gentleman, though they say he is a hard landlord and that his tenants hold no love for him.

Miss Martha married a clergyman from the north of the county. He is the second son of a baronet near Ripon. And so the family trouble, which came to light with the reading of George Holmes's will, was smoothed over, as such troubles often are.

The will?

You ask a lot of an old woman's memory. Let me think. Yes, Heslington was mentioned there. Can you believe it – the old man left him one third of his estate! One third to Mr James, one third to Miss Martha and one third to the bastard child, as it turned out. Heslington was George Holmes's son by the housekeeper, who played a close game until she could contain it no more and the secret came out. Mrs Holmes never recovered from the revelation, poor lady.

And no, Heslington did not return to claim his inheritance. I doubt he ever knew of it, or of his parentage.

The housekeeper did say however, in a last letter to Mrs Holmes, that it was she who had witnessed George Holmes's death. Lest anyone else be blamed, she confessed that she had forced the meeting at midnight in the library to insist that he put a stop once and for all to Miss Martha's flirting with Heslington.

The old man could not endure the difficulties of the situation as she presented it to him. It seems he fell dead from a heart attack and she withdrew before Mr James appeared on the scene.

So there was an end to it.

No, Emily did not speak of it, as I recall. She learned more about it than most, but she would not share what she knew.

As for what followed – it was one or two years after this that Branwell tried for an artist in London, but he did not make anything of himself.

However, the games the girls played in childhood paid off in the end – the stories about heroes and heroines, about battles and exile. They wrote books for grown men and women at last, and had them published, though Emily and Anne had little enough time to enjoy their fame.

Emily died of consumption in December of 1848. Anne followed her in May the next year.

Charlotte lives still, God bless her, and is to be married to Mr Brontë's curate later this summer.

But then, I only tell you what you know, for what else brings you here?